Incredible
People

Incredible

Five Stories of Extraordinary Lives

People

Frederick Drimmer

ATHENEUM BOOKS FOR YOUNG READERS

For BiBi and DiDi
with love

Atheneum Books for Young Readers
An imprint of Simon & Schuster Children's Publishing Division
1230 Avenue of the Americas
New York, New York 10020

Book design by Ethan Trask
The text of this book is set in Mrs. Eaves.

First Edition
Printed in the United States of America
10 9 8 7 6 5 4 3 2 1

Library of Congress Cataloging-in-Publication Data
Drimmer, Frederick.
Incredible people : five stories of extraordinary lives / by Frederick Drimmer.
p. cm.
Includes bibliographical references (p.) and index.
Summary: Presents the stories of six people whose lives were shaped by their physical and cultural differences from the rest of Western society: Jack Erlich, the Hilton Siamese twins, Ota Benga, Ishi, and the "Wild Boy" of France.
ISBN 0-689-31921-5
1. Biography—Juvenile literature. 2. Abnormalities, Human—Biography—Juvenile literature. [1. Biography. 2. Abnormalities, Human—Biography. 3. Curiosities and wonders.] I. Title.
CT107.D75 1997
920'.02—dc20
96-9082

Contents

Can such things be . . .
without our special wonder?

William Shakespeare, *Macbeth*

■

In the depth of winter,
I finally learned that within me
there lay an invincible summer.

Albert Camus

Acknowledgments

A book like this may have only one author, but many contribute to it. Making acknowledgment for great help generously provided while this project was in the making is one of the most pleasurable duties of its author.

To Marcia Marshall, my editor, I owe more than I can say for her interest and encouragement all along the way.

Leonor De La Vega, Jill Blake, and the Harry Hertzberg Circus Collection and Museum of San Antonio, Texas, provided photographs and reference material as well as aid and comfort during my stay in their city.

Wayne Daniel, librarian of the Southwest Collection of the El Paso Public Library, El Paso, Texas, furnished advice and reference material about Jack Earle and his family. So did Fred Dahlinger Jr., director of the Robert L. Parkinson Library and Research Center of the Circus World Museum, Baraboo, Wisconsin, where I have spent many fascinating hours.

Rosemary J. Lands of the Robinson-Spangler Carolina Room of the Public Library of Charlotte and Mecklenburg County, Charlotte, North Carolina, dug into her hoard of information about the Hilton sisters to enlighten me about the years they spent in her city. Dr. Joyce Schwartz of the Department of Pathology, University of Texas, San Antonio, patiently researched the latest information about Siamese twins and shared with me her lifelong enthusiasm for the circus.

Anne Prah-Perochon, editor of *Journal Français d'Amérique,* San

Francisco, explained at length certain facets of the life of the wild boy of Aveyron. John Francis Iaderosa, curator of the New York Zoological Society, and the society's library helped me with background material about Ota Benga's stay at the Bronx Zoo. And I am permanently in debt to John H. Hurdle, former curator of the Ringling Museum of the Circus in Sarasota, Florida, for his general guidance and wisdom.

Gaby Monet of Home Box Office, New York City, generously made available still photographs from the television motion picture *Some Call Them Freaks*, which I wrote for HBO and she produced and directed.

The staffs of a number of libraries have been enormously helpful in supplying reference material: the Billy Rose Theater Collection of the Library of Performing Arts, New York City; the library of the New York Academy of Medicine; and the public libraries of Norwalk, Wilton, Westport, Greenwich, and Old Greenwich (particularly Barbara Bojonell) in Connecticut, as well as the central branch of the New York Public Library.

For their enthusiastic support and encouragement I am grateful to Amelia, Andrew, and Jean Iaderosa, Barbara Osborn and John Drimmer, and Rosaria and Anatole Konstantin.

My wife, Evelyn, reference librarian of the Perrot Memorial Library of Old Greenwich, worked devotedly to obtain a multitude of books and a small mountain of information from libraries and other institutions throughout the United States. Although last on this list, she knows she is forever first with me.

Frederick Drimmer

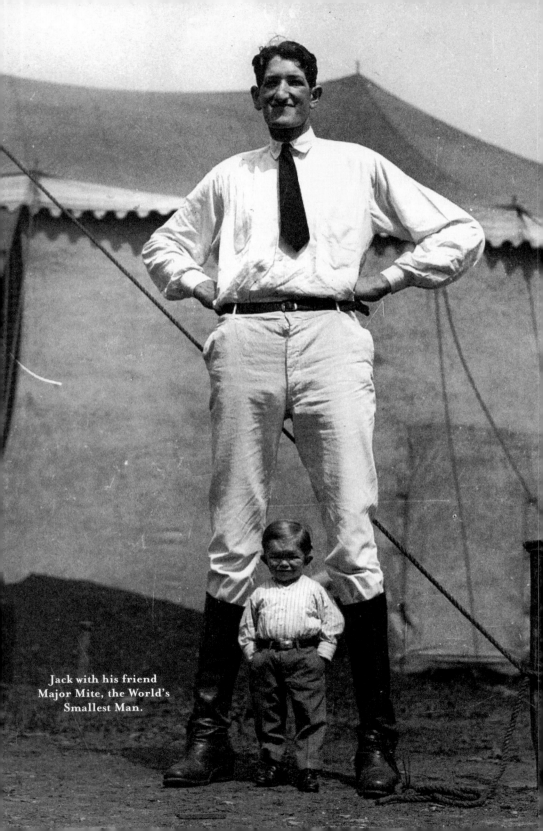

Jack with his friend
Major Mite, the World's
Smallest Man.

The Gentle Giant

He was born in Denver in June 1906. At birth he was a little thing, smaller than most babies, weighing only three pounds twelve ounces. He was so tiny and frail that his distraught mother and father were afraid he wouldn't live. They kept running to the baby's crib to make sure he was still breathing.

They named him Jacob. Year by year he grew, but very slowly. The parents, Dora and Isadore Erlich, were always looking at the neighbors' children, comparing them to their little son, and always he was the smallest. Below average height themselves, they kept telling each other there was nothing to worry about. But they weren't entirely convinced.

Until he turned seven.

All at once little Jacob began to shoot upward. Almost every month he looked an inch taller. His rate of growth was prodigious.

Earlier the Erlichs hadn't had to spend a penny on clothing for him; he had a big brother, and he could always wear things the older boy had outgrown. After six months, however, that was ancient history. Before the year was out, Jacob's parents were buying him completely new outfits—including shoes not just the size a full-grown man wears, but the biggest man's size they could find.

The family moved to Texas, to El Paso, where Isadore opened a jewelry shop. Before the boy turned ten *he was more than six feet tall.* His feet were so large now, no store carried shoes that would fit him: his footwear had to be made to order. That cost big bucks.

At the start, the Erlichs couldn't have been happier to see their son add another inch or another pound to his once undersized body. But already they had something new to worry about.

Jacob, after being too small for his age, had become too big. He was beginning to look . . . abnormal.

His anxious parents took him to the doctor. What's the matter with the boy? they asked. When will he stop growing? The doctor scratched his chin. He couldn't offer any explanation.

They took him to another doctor, and another. Each was as puzzled as the one before. They simply had never seen a case like this.

If the Erlichs were troubled by Jacob's extraordinary growth, their worries were nothing next to his.

The changes the boy was seeing in his body terrified him. His arms were growing incredibly long, like an ape's, and his legs long and spindly. His hands and feet were becoming huge. His nose and chin were massive, way out of proportion to the rest of his face. Every time he saw himself in a mirror he got a shock.

Something terrible was wrong with him, he was sure.

When Jacob could no longer keep his worries to himself, he poured them out to his parents. They smiled and did their best to reassure him, but he could see the tension in their faces. The smiles were forced. They needed reassurance almost as much as he did.

As if the bizarre things happening to the boy weren't bad enough, he had another worry—the way his changed appearance was affecting everyone who saw him.

Especially the boys and girls he went to school with. Children can be cruel. They have little tolerance for someone very different from themselves. Looking at the giant boy, they couldn't resist making fun of him.

Some of his schoolmates got a kick out of calling him Pecos Bill.

Pecos Bill is a legendary giant cowboy of Texas folklore. All sorts of unbelievable feats have been credited to Pecos Bill. For example, one year it was extremely dry, and Pecos Bill had to lug water from the far-off Gulf of Mexico. After a while he got tired of this: there had to be a better way to get the water. He solved the problem by digging an eighteen-hundred-mile canal up from the gulf, all the way through Texas. It took him just a day to dig—he was a giant, after all. As the water flowed through the canal, it looked like a big river to him, so he named it the Rio Grande, which means "Big River" in Spanish.

A tall story about a supertall man. Pretty funny, you might think—but it wasn't funny to a sensitive boy, made even more sensitive by the constant teasing. Jacob also had to get used to hearing himself called by a string of other nicknames; "Old Highpockets" and "Giraffe" were two of the nicer ones.

For the young giant, just walking through the schoolyard could be hell. Sometimes he felt like an Indian running a gauntlet. Hoots and jeers pelted him constantly, and they bruised him worse than blows.

On his way to or from school, the boy was careful to choose a little-used street or alleyway—and to hurry down it as fast as his long legs would carry him. When he saw another child approaching, he'd squeeze into a dark doorway; he'd try to make himself as small as possible, waiting until the footsteps died away.

In 1919 Jacob turned thirteen. He stood more than seven feet tall in his stocking feet. Although he didn't know it, *he was the tallest boy in America.*

No one understood Jacob's heartaches better than his father and mother. One day Isadore asked the gangling giant if he'd like to join him on a trip to Los Angeles and go deep-sea fishing. The offer brought a whoop of joy from the boy.

On the long train ride, Isadore couldn't help notice the other passengers staring at his son or murmuring to one another about him. How poor Jake must suffer, he thought.

Finally they arrived in Los Angeles. They would need to buy some tackle, the elder Erlich informed the younger, and he asked him to come along. They walked through street after street packed with people, searching for a suitable fishing-equipment shop.

Everywhere they went, people kept stopping and turning to get a better look at the odd pair—the enormous boy and his small father. Some smiled; a few laughed out loud.

After a time, Jacob noticed he and his father were passing a particular fishing-equipment shop for the third time. He pointed this out to Isadore. Couldn't they go inside and get the tackle now?

Isadore replied with a question. It astonished the boy.

"Jake," his father asked, "do you still mind the people?"

The boy had been exposed to more curious glances that day than at any other time in his life. He thought for a moment. "No, not anymore."

"All right. I want you to remember that people aren't laughing *at* you. They're laughing *with* you."

Somehow Jacob wasn't convinced. But he could see how hard his good-hearted father was striving to help. He would remember Isadore's words as long as he lived.

Word about the seven-foot-plus youngster spread rapidly across the city. Not long after, at the end of a day of fishing, Jacob and his father were pulling up to the dock. There they found two men waiting for them expectantly.

The men introduced themselves: Zion Meyers and Jerry Ash of

Century Studios, a Hollywood movie company. They'd heard about the boy giant, they said, and wanted to see him for themselves.

They must have liked what they saw. One pulled out a sheaf of papers and placed it in Isadore's hands. He turned over the pages, frowning with concentration. Jake read it too, stooping.

It was a contract for the boy to act in motion pictures.

Going to the movies was a big event in Jake's life. (It was in just about everybody's, in the days before television.) Century Studios actually wanted to make him a movie actor!

Jake couldn't believe it.

His father was hugging him. He took the contract from Isadore's hand and read it over again, this time more carefully.

Yes, there it was in black and white. It was real.

A movie actor!

He was thrilled right down to his faraway toes.

Century Studios gave the young giant more than a profession. It gave him a new name. No longer would he be Jake Erlich. Henceforth he would be known as Jack Earle.

No longer would he have to stoop or try to shrink to avoid attracting attention. From now on, the taller he grew, the more the studio would like it.

For the first time in his life he was surrounded by people who looked up to him—and not just in a physical sense. The other actors, the camera crew, all the studio people admired and respected him.

In his hometown too his new career made a striking difference in the way people viewed him. El Pasoans exclaimed with wonder and delight when they saw movie publicity shots of the giant so many of them had laughed at.

One picture they chuckled over showed Jack sporting a mustache—

not a real one, of course—and fashionably dressed. He was straddling an automobile wheel with his long legs, and filling the tank with gasoline with one hand while turning the crank with the other. (In those days automobiles had to be cranked to start.) Yes, that was our Jake—or Jack.

Suddenly he was a celebrity to the home folks. People were proud to say they knew him. El Paso newspapers regularly ran articles about him, telling how tall he was at last report, his giant roles, where his latest movie could be seen.

"Talkies"—moving pictures like those we see today, in which we hear the voices of the people on the screen and the sounds of the action—were still some years away when Jack arrived in Hollywood. He was a featured player in a long series of silent two-reel comedies Century was filming in its studios on Sunset Boulevard.

Century had signed up a new child star, Peggy Montgomery, whom it called "Baby Peggy." The Shirley Temple of the 1920s, Peggy was under three when she was discovered. The tiny tot's bold carryings-on in episode after episode at the head of a cast of child actors won her great popularity. As for Jack, the contrast between his size and that of the other youngsters would send audiences into hysterics.

One of his first roles, in 1922, when he was sixteen, was in *Jack and the Beanstalk*. He was seven feet three inches tall, and weighed 237 pounds. Naturally he played the wicked giant.

A publicity shot showed him in his fairy-tale giant's costume, with a mustache and beard circling his mouth and the meanest of mean expressions on his face. He was standing in front of a house, the top of its doorway below his shoulders. Clutching one of his enormous boots for dear life with her arms and legs, her face upturned with a pitiful, pleading look, was tiny Baby Peggy.

He was already working on his next movie, *Moonshiners,* being filmed in Yosemite Valley, the accompanying article in his hometown newspaper reported. When he bought his railroad ticket he asked for a lower berth.

"I haven't one," the clerk said. "Will you take an upper?"

"I don't know whether I can get into one," Jack replied. "I'll try."

A porter took him to a sleeping car. Jack found he could sit on the edge of the upper berth by sticking his head out through the ventilator. He could lie down by wrapping both legs around his neck.

I'll sit up all night, he decided, and went off in search of a seat.

Early in his Hollywood career Jack discovered that the average man will treat someone bigger than himself with respect.

One day he was in an open car with Meyers, driving in Los Angeles. Traffic was heavy, and the Meyers car nicked the fender of a big black limousine.

Both cars stopped. The limousine driver, a tough-faced man in a chauffeur's uniform, got out, looked at the damage, cursed, and came over to Meyers. Hands balled, face black with anger, he ordered Meyers to step on the sidewalk and face him like a man.

Meyers turned pale. He poked Jack in the ribs. "Stand up!" he said in a whisper. "Stand up!"

Jack, puzzled, remained in his seat.

The furious chauffeur yanked at the door handle, growling.

"Stand up, you big idiot!" hissed Meyers to Jack, poking him harder.

The giant got the message at last. Slowly he unwound his great body and stood up.

The chauffeur stared. He shook his head. "Pardon me." He backed off and returned to the limousine. "All my fault. Sorry."

For two years Jack played in comedies for Century. In 1923, when he reached seventeen, he was seven feet six and one-half inches tall. On the movie set he was having the time of his life.

Things were very different, however, when he left the studio. In his bed, at night, he was haunted by nightmares.

When would he stop growing? What would happen if he didn't? No one would or could give him the answers.

The future terrified him.

What becomes of child actors when they grow out of childhood? The lucky ones, like Elizabeth Taylor or Jodie Foster, go on to mature roles and remain stars all their lives. But, for most, the roles become scarcer and scarcer as the young players lose the special childlike qualities that endeared them to the public. After a time they vanish from the screen.*

Jack would disappear from the screen too, but for a very different reason. The end of his movie career came suddenly and disastrously. So disastrously that his life could have ended with it.

The giant, at seventeen, was acting in his forty-ninth comedy. He was standing atop a lofty scaffolding when he felt it tremble. It gave way. Down and down he went, plunging to the ground below. Some of the scaffolding landed on him.

Everything went black.

When Jack came to, he was lying on a hospital bed. His body ached all over. Especially his head.

His nose was throbbing. He raised his hand to it. It was buried under a mound of bandages. (It was broken.)

Most disturbing of all, his eyesight was blurred.

---

*Baby Peggy herself shared this fate. After her movie career ended, she became a writer under the name of Diana Serra Cary. Her book *Hollywood's Children* (1978) tells the story of child movie actors, including herself. A film with the same title, available on video, was based on it.

Next day, Jack's vision hadn't improved. It was growing dimmer.

On the third day, opening his eyes, he had the fright of his life. He was completely blind.

The boy's stricken parents took him home to El Paso. X rays of his skull revealed an abnormal shape on his pituitary gland. It was a tumor. It must have been there for years, but it had never been detected before. When he crashed down with the scaffolding, the tumor was driven up against his optic nerve. The pressure had made him lose his sight.

X rays, the doctors told the Erlichs, might help. So time and again they took their sightless, helpless son to the hospital, and waited while the invisible fingers of the big X-ray machine went to work.

It was like a miracle. Little by little the tumor was shrinking.

At the end of four months the boy could see as well as ever.

During the four years he'd been in Hollywood, Jack had been attending school, as the law required. Now he enrolled in college.

As the months went by, he noticed something peculiar was happening to him.

Earlier, he'd always begun to outgrow his clothing almost as soon as it was ordered. Now, after months of wear, his shirts, his trousers, his jackets, and other garments seemed to fit him as well as ever. His shoes, instead of starting to pinch, continued to feel comfortable.

He told his parents. Excited, they ran for the tape measure.

He was still the same height he'd been months ago, before the accident!

Why had he stopped growing? No one could say. Jack became convinced that the tumor on his pituitary gland had been responsible for his incredible growth—and, after the X rays had shrunk it, could no longer make him grow.

In the 1920s our knowledge of the endocrine system—of which the pituitary gland is an important part—was still in its infancy. Today we know that Jack's hunch was correct. The normal pituitary, located at the base of the brain, secretes growth hormones, and these cause our long bones to grow normally. If, for some unexplained reason, however, a tumor forms on the gland, the tumor can stimulate it to produce an abnormally large quantity of these hormones. The result is a pathological giant.

With his tumor X-rayed out of existence, Jack would grow no more. He would remain permanently seven feet six and one-half inches tall.

X-ray treatment to arrest abnormal growth was unknown in Jack's time (although it was being used to shrink tumors). If the accident that led to his treatment had never happened, he would have kept growing, until some complication led to his early death. This is what happened to the tallest man who ever lived, whom we shall meet later.*

A few more words about giants are in order here. First, we should answer the question: What is a giant? Generally it's a person who is unusually tall—6 feet 6.7 inches or more in men; in women, 6 feet 1.6 inches. Giants are by no means always abnormal, or pathological. Most, in fact, are normal—people who are unusually tall because their parents are.

Giants may also owe their height to their race. A famous example is the Watusi (or Tutsi) of Africa, a very tall, slender people in Burundi and Rwanda.

While Jack was attending college in El Paso, "the Greatest Show on Earth"—the Ringling Brothers and Barnum & Bailey Circus—came to

---

*Surgery is also used now to halt abnormal growth. The tallest woman in America today, Sandy Allen (seven feet seven inches tall), had a pituitary tumor removed surgically in 1977, arresting further growth. Unfortunately, although medical science can make a pathological giant stop growing, there is no way to make one shorter.

town. In its sideshow* it featured a giant who was billed as "the Tallest Man on Earth." (Any giant the circus featured was advertised by that title, just as the midget it featured was called "the Smallest Man on Earth.") Ringling's Tallest Man on Earth at that time was Jim Tarver, known as "the Texas Giant." According to advertisements—which were always exaggerated—he was seven feet five inches tall.

In the days before television, the annual arrival of the circus in a town was one of the biggest events of the year in an entertainment-hungry America. Among the hordes who crowded into the sideshow tent were some of Jack's classmates. Seeing Jim Tarver, every one of them was ready to bet Jack was taller.

Come to the circus with us, his friends pleaded with him. We'll show them a *real* giant.

Jack wasn't wild about the idea. But his friends insisted, and he finally said yes.

One look at Tarver and Jack had to agree with his friends. According to reports, the Texas Giant himself was impressed.

Jim Tarver was the circus's Tallest Man on Earth until Jack came along. With him is Major Mite, the World's Smallest Man.

---

*A sideshow, in the circus, was an extra show in which human oddities ("freaks") and other performers, like sword-swallowers and fire-eaters, were exhibited. Circuses in the United States no longer have sideshows. Some may still be seen at carnivals and state fairs, but they have become rare. The exhibition of deformed or handicapped human beings, once extremely popular, is considered degrading nowadays, and is prohibited in some states.

Next day a stranger showed up at Isadore Erlich's jewelry store, but he wasn't looking for jewelry. He was from Ringling Brothers. The jeweler's son could have a wonderful job as a circus giant, he said. Good pay, easy work, a chance to see the USA. A rare opportunity. The circus was ready to offer a contract.

That evening the Erlichs went into a huddle. This time it was Jack who was opposed.

If he joined the circus, he said, he'd have to be part of the sideshow. What kind of people appeared in the sideshow? *Freaks.* He'd been there and he'd seen it. He didn't want any part of it.

Jack's father, by contrast, was all for accepting the offer. They argued. Neither could convince the other. Finally they decided to ask the family doctor's opinion.

The doctor sided with Isadore. No reason why Jack shouldn't sign up with Ringling, he said—and some good reasons why he should.

The doctor had observed the boy seemed moody at times. Jack, he believed, missed the glamour and excitement of acting in Hollywood. The circus, the physician thought, could give all of that back to him and more. On the physical side, he could see no objections. The boy had recovered completely from his injuries. The change was bound to do him good.

Jack's father nodded vigorously. "Being a freak," he said, "is only a state of mind." According to an old saying, "As a man thinketh, so is he." If Jack didn't *think* of himself as a freak, he would never be one. In the circus, just as in the movies, his great height would give him not just an unusual career but a renewed sense of worth.

Father and son argued back and forth. In the end they compromised: Jack would go with the circus—but just for a single year. If things didn't work out in that time he would leave and go back to school.

The Gentle Giant

Ringling traveled from city to city on its own train. With its vast and varied equipment stowed carefully away, with its elephants, lions, tigers, and other animals, and its hundreds of performers and workers all in their own special cars (more than seventy of them, each one double the usual length), the circus made ready to leave El Paso.

At the railroad station Jack stooped over to give his two small parents a last, tearful hug. They hugged him back. They watched with aching hearts as their giant boy climbed aboard the sideshow train. They read the number on its side: 96. They would see it in their dreams.

Circus people are a hearty, boisterous lot. The noise inside Car 96 was deafening. Confused, unsure of himself, Jack looked nervously around.

In one of the seats he recognized his fellow giant, Jim Tarver. Jack had already gotten to know some of the midgets—perfectly formed little people, no larger than children—and they called out to him warmly in their tiny, high-pitched voices. The two fat ladies—they weighed upward of four or five hundred pounds—greeted the shy stranger with motherly words. A woman with startlingly white hair and pale pink eyes (she was an albino) was chatting with Eko and Iko, who were known as "the Ambassadors from Mars"; the circus said they had come to Earth on a spaceship. They had long blond curls and beards, but were actually albino African Americans.

Jack found an empty seat and looked around some more. Among his companions he recognized a man so thin he was called a living skeleton, a woman covered all over her body (except for her pretty face) with tattoos of every imaginable color and description, as well as a sword-swallower, a fire-eater, a bearded lady, and Clicko, the famous little yellow-skinned dancing Bushman from Africa.

Outside, a steam whistle blew, sharp and shrill. The long train lurched and it got under way. Looking out of the window, Jack watched the twinkling lights of the city disappear behind.

Never had he felt so alone as he did now, in the midst of all these strangers. Some of them looked so odd, he thought they might actually have come from outer space.

He himself, he was certain, was the oddest of all.

After a while the seats in the car began to empty; the sideshow people were heading for their bunks. Jack went to his own, swung himself inside, and drew the curtain.

The bunk was a double one, to accommodate his great body. Even so, it felt small after his big special bed at home. A feeling of anxiety swept over him, one he felt whenever he found himself in a space too small for comfort. (Psychologists call this "claustrophobia.")

Nearby he heard people snoring in their bunks. Would he ever fall asleep?

Jack was a giant—but inside his giant's body there was a little child. (There is in every one of us.) That little child lay awake that night for hours, missing his mother and father, his brothers. He missed his quiet room, his bed, his home, all the things that were so familiar and comfortable.

How would he get along with these strange people in this strange new world? Would he find friends among them? (It was always so hard for him to make friends.)

Under the warm blankets he began to shiver.

Circus life was completely new to Jack. But show business wasn't. In Hollywood, the clothing Jack had worn and the sets he'd acted on were often contrived to make him look bigger. In the sideshow, his costumes and his footwear were carefully chosen to add inches to his great height.

In New York City the Ringling Brothers and Barnum & Bailey Circus always appeared in Madison Square Garden. (It still does.) The sideshow had its own showplace in the basement. There, in the fall of 1926, for the first time, Jack discovered what it was really like to be a circus giant.

In the dressing room he looked in the mirror. He had never seen anything as outlandish as the costume he had to wear now. What was he supposed to be—a cossack or a prince? He glittered with gold braid, gold buttons, gold epaulets, and shone with patent leather. His headpiece, of red satin, was a good sixteen inches high. Platform shoes added to his height.

"I had to keep moving my toes to make sure those were my own feet down below," he said.

Circus advertisements added close to a foot to his height; they said that he was eight feet six inches tall. And in this costume he really looked it.

The members of the sideshow took their positions next to one another on two platforms, one higher and slightly behind the other. The thirty-odd performers (performers was what they liked to call themselves) were given specific positions, half on one platform, half on the other. Jack's position was on the upper platform. (That made him look still taller.)

Suddenly the word "Doors!" rang out. It was the signal that the sideshow was about to begin. The doors swung open, and hundreds and hundreds of eager circusgoers, many of them mothers and fathers with their children, poured in. They crowded along the front of the lower platform.

Ringling Brothers' sideshow troupe in 1933, with Jack in the middle. Major
Mite stands next to him; Harry Doll is third from left. In the bottom row,
second from left, is Frank Lentini, who had three legs. The two men with
long curls are Eko and Iko, the Ambassadors from Mars.

Jack looked down at the vast sea of faces gazing up. To him it seemed
that the eyes of every single person were fixed upon him.

He felt giddy. His cheeks flushed. His heart was pounding. A powerful urge to leap down to the floor and run away took hold of him.

"Take it easy, Jack."

The voice was tiny and high, like a child's. It seemed to come from
beneath his feet.

On the platform below, a little man, dressed to the nines in a tuxe-
do and a top hat, was smiling up at him. It was Harry Doll, one of the
midgets.

"Don't worry, Jack!" piped Harry. He winked. "There are more
freaks out in the crowd than there are up here."

A warm feeling flooded through the giant. Somebody realized what he was going through—and cared enough to utter those reassuring words! He smiled wanly, and gradually he calmed down. Never would he forget what the midget had said; in fact, he would soon become fast friends with Harry and his little troupe, his three lovely midget sisters, Daisy, Tiny, and Grace. One of the best-known families of little people in show business, the Dolls were from Germany. (In time they would thank their lucky stars they had left that country when they did.) They had changed their name from Schneider to Doll, one that was much more fitting for people their size, and they billed themselves as "the Dancing Dolls."*

A contrast in sizes: Jack Earle and his fellow circus star Harry Doll

Jack would make other friends in the circus. But his closest ones would always be the little people. The opposite ends of the human scale—the extremely tall and the extremely short—seemed to feel a natural attraction toward each other. Perhaps that was because they were usually paired in the sideshow, appearing side by side on the platform. Not only that: the circus frequently asked its giants to pose

---

*The Dolls would appear in a number of well-known motion pictures, among them *Good News, The Wizard of Oz,* (as Munchkins), and *Freaks,* a famous horror movie in which Harry would star. The Hilton twins, whose story is told elsewhere in this book, were featured players in the film.

with the little people for publicity shots. There was a good reason for this: the contrast between the great height of the giants and the minuteness of the midgets could always be counted on to make newsworthy photographs.

Time and time again, circus photographers would ask Jack to pick up one of his little friends and hold that tiny person on one of his thirteen-inch hands. Among those who posed with him were Harry Doll (for one photograph Harry and two of his sisters sat on Jack's arm), Major Mite (two feet two inches tall, one of the shortest men ever to be featured by the sideshow), and Lia Graf, an attractive German midget.

Lia won international fame when a circus publicity man plumped her down unexpectedly in the lap of one of the richest men in the world—the financier J. P. Morgan—and a camera recorded the event. This happened in Washington, D.C., as the scowling tycoon was waiting to answer the questions of the United States Senate Banking Committee. The photograph of the midget and the startled millionaire made the front pages of newspapers around the globe.*

Circus publicity agents got publicity in many ways. In 1936, when the circus was opening in Madison Square Garden, they called in the press to interview Jack about his paintings. Yes, Jack was a painter (as well as a sculptor), and his pictures were being exhibited at a gallery in El Paso. The *New York Herald-Tribune* called him "the cultured giant of Ringling Brothers."

Every year, when the circus season closed for the winter, the giant

---

*Some years later, Lia went home to Germany. It was a fatal error. Adolf Hitler, who came to power in 1933, soon began his campaign to exterminate the Jews, as well as human oddities of every kind. Lia had the bad luck to be not only a human oddity but a Jew also. In 1937 the Gestapo arrested her. In 1941 she and her mother and father disappeared into the gas chambers of Auschwitz.

went home to his folks in El Paso. There he plunged into his art.

Earlier he had been painting scenes of the Texas desert. On the advice of a local artist who gave him lessons, he turned to another subject: the circus. He painted circus scenes, moods, personalities—the elephants, the clowns, the midgets, the circus on the move.

One of his pictures showed the midway on the circus grounds.

"In *The Midway*," he told an interviewer, "I have tried to catch the impression of the crowd—heat, music, children crying, and the cries of the ballyhoo men."

Over the throngs in the midway the bright flags were blowing from the white tent tops. In front of the sideshow there were posters with pictures of Jack, the fat lady, others—pictures within a picture.

"I have so many ideas," Jack said, "they are crowding in on my sleep at night. It's a wonderful feeling. . . . I want to do the midgets sitting at a meal and arguing, as only they can argue."

Lia Graf, a German midget, was an attractive handful for the Texas Giant. She would perish in the gas chamber at Auschwitz.

Besides painting—his many pictures splashed the walls of his parents' home—he read, saw friends, and took part in community activities. He was a celebrity, called upon to lead parades and community drives.

Every March his painting ended. He had to be off to join the circus in Florida, for the new season was about to begin. He would have to wait till his next vacation to find time for art.

As a circus giant Jack made a good living. In addition to his salary, he earned money from extras: he sold photographs of himself and a replica of his finger ring—which was big enough for a half-dollar to pass through. A genuine giant's ring for twenty-five cents was a good buy, and he sold thousands. They were called lucky rings—and certainly they were lucky for Jack, since they cost him very little.*

People often wonder how much a giant has to eat to provide strength and energy for his enormous frame. We don't have to guess about Jack's appetite, for we have the eyewitness testimony of an old circus hand, Albert Tucker, who was a good friend.

"His appetite was terrific," Tucker said. "I recall one time when we had just completed a full meal, from soup to dessert. Jack called the waitress and ordered a thick T-bone steak with a double order of home-fried potatoes. The waitress thought that he was 'ribbing,' but he assured her that the first meal was only an appetizer. Then he proceeded to put away the steak and finished the meal with a huge slice of apple pie topped with a heaping scoop of ice cream."

You'll sometimes see a giant referred to as "gentle." The adjective certainly fitted Jack. So far as we know, he was involved in a fight only once in his adult life. That occurred when the circus was playing in Chattanooga, and Jack was strolling down the midway, just a few steps behind his buddy Harry Doll.

Human oddities have to put up with abuse from so-called "normals,"

---

*One of these rings is in the collection of the Ringling Brothers Circus Museum in Sarasota, Florida. In later years, when Jack came across someone who had bought one of his rings, he offered to return the price with interest because they tarnished quickly and there was nothing marvelous about them except their size. But the purchasers insisted the rings had really brought them luck and refused to part with them!

who sometimes appear to feel that anybody who is different is fair game for them. In this instance, a local man reached out his hand toward Harry; he looked as if he intended to play some unpleasant trick on the midget.

The man's movement and the expression on his face didn't escape Jack's eye. His fist shot out and slammed against the bully's chin. Then he wrapped the troublemaker in his great arms (he had a "wing-spread" of seven feet four inches, we are told) and spun him around, giving him a good shaking.

His jaw fractured, the man was taken to the hospital. Later he brought a lawsuit against the circus. After that, Jack made a special point of avoiding fights.

Jack had good times in the circus, but with the years he became increasingly unhappy. He could never forget how he'd reacted when the first circus contract was offered to him: he hadn't wanted to sign up because he didn't want to be looked upon as a freak. But that, he felt more and more, was what being in the sideshow made him.

He took no pleasure in standing solemnly on the sideshow plat-form, as he was required to do during every performance, to be stared at by the crowds while a showman talked about his physical peculiari-ties. He felt ridiculous in his cowboy costume, with the high-heeled boots and the tall Stetson hat, or his Buckingham Palace guardsman's uniform, with the lofty bearskin headpiece, or the other outfits he had to wear to exaggerate his height. Oh, he could manage a smile posing with Major Mite or some other little mite in his hand, or leaning on an elephant and towering over it. (Actually it was a baby elephant.) He was a bookish, artistic person and, as we have seen, extremely sensitive. Making a spectacle of himself nauseated him.

He felt ridiculous when he walked through the audience with his arms outstretched, something a giant was expected to do. ("There was seldom a man or woman who would have to duck," the circus barker Harry Lewiston would write later.) As Jack made his way through the crowd, some suspicious boy was likely to kick him in the shins to see if he really was that tall or just a much shorter person standing on stilts. Grown men too would try to pick fights with him after they'd had too much to drink.

Was Jack really taller than an elephant? Well, a baby elephant.

Then there were the endless questions he had to listen to over and over again—questions like how big was the bed he slept in, how much more did he eat than ordinary people, or why was he a giant.* When he wasn't being bored to death answering queries like these, he was grappling with others that were embarrassing or downright rude.

When "the Tall Texan" (one of the names bestowed on Jack by the circus) was introduced to people, they would frequently ask him, "How's the weather up there?" This, they appeared to think, was extremely funny. It wasn't to Jack—at least not after the first few thousand times he heard it. "I used to swear I'd murder the next man who asked me that," he said.

---

*Sandy Allen, America's tallest woman, when she was in show business used to take a good-humored revenge on questioners by wearing a T-shirt with the words "Why are you so short?"

The Gentle Giant

Life is full of curious inconsistencies. Once Jack suffered an acute attack of embarrassment when he realized he'd just asked somebody the very same question. The person he asked was actually the giant of giants—Robert Wadlow, the tallest man who ever lived.*

Young Robert, sometimes called "the Alton Giant," would eventually reach a height of 8 feet II.I inches. (His astonishing story is told in the author's book *Very Special People*.) Like Jack, Robert was a pathological giant. The two were introduced in Chicago. Jack, who had never met anybody taller than himself, was momentarily speechless. Automatically, the hated words came from his lips: "Hey, Bob, how's the weather up there?"

Robert, still a boy, was thrilled to meet a real circus giant, and took the

Robert Wadlow, 8 feet II.I inches tall, the tallest man who ever lived. He appeared in the circus with Jack in 1937.

remark with a good grace. Not so Jack. The instant he realized what he'd said, a deep flush spread over his face.

(Long after Jack had left the circus he continued to be asked the same question. But by then he had learned the lesson of tolerance. "I don't really mind it anymore," he said. "I can even shoot back an answer: 'Hot air at the summit, somewhat cooler in the foothills.'")

■ ■ ■

*Many others have laid claim to this title; Robert, however, is the only one whose height was certified by medical authorities, who measured him at the Washington University School of Medicine in St. Louis.

One day, at the end of the show in Madison Square Garden, Jack was approached by a well-dressed young woman. She had a worried look on her face. She had a small son, she said anxiously, whose life had been made miserable by a governess who kept telling him frightening stories of wicked giants. Sometimes she had threatened that if he didn't obey her, she'd call a giant to punish him. As a result, the boy was in a constant state of anxiety.*

"Won't you please talk to him?" the young mother begged Jack. "I know you can help."

He was happy to. Taking a few of his midget friends along to back him up, Jack succeeded in convincing the boy that he was a good giant, and that real giants were no different from anybody else. Jack, who was particularly fond of children, kept up a correspondence with the boy for a long time.

"I haven't heard from him in many years," Jack once told an interviewer, "but I know he's married and has children." He smiled wryly. "Undoubtedly he's now frightening his own kids with stories about giants."

Still, Jack had done *his* bit to fight the myth that giants are to be feared.

As the 1930s drew to an end, Jack found life as a sideshow giant increasingly unbearable. He was earning a living, and a fairly good one at that, at a time when millions of his fellow Americans were jobless

---

*Giants, like dwarfs, have traditionally been portrayed in a bad light in folklore and in literature. Among the most wicked were the terrible one-eyed Cyclops, slain by Ulysses in Homer's *Odyssey,* and the Philistine giant Goliath, who was felled by a stone from the slingshot of the young shepherd David in the Bible. The fee-fi-fo-fum giant in the tale of Jack and the Beanstalk is still a frightening figure to small children. (As we saw earlier, Jack played the role of this giant when he was acting in Hollywood.)

and many went to bed hungry. (Later this time would be called the Great Depression.) But he felt he couldn't go on much longer.

Jack's constitution wasn't too strong either. Pathological giants aren't the healthiest of people. The strain of being constantly on the move, of opening in new towns, sometimes every day, and the long hours inside the hot tent, wore him down. Often he felt close to cracking up.

"There were times when I wished I had never been born," he would say. "I hated the world."

The end came on a winter's day in 1940. The season had just closed, and the circus was in Tampa. "All the glamour and color had ended for me," he would say.

In fairy tales and literature, giants are usually pictured as cruel ogres, sometimes with a taste for human flesh.

Hunting up the manager, Jack told him he was through. Next spring, when the circus opened, somebody else would have to stand on the sideshow platform in front of the goggle-eyed crowds and be the Tallest Man on Earth.

When you're in your mid-thirties, it hurts to realize you've spent fourteen years—close to half of your life—in the wrong kind of job. It hurts even more to realize you will have to start all over again—to find something to do that has real meaning for you. Jack was deeply depressed.

That year a world's fair, the Golden Gate International Exposition, was held on Treasure Island in San Francisco Bay. The giant was wandering through the crowds when he saw a face that looked familiar. It belonged to Art Linkletter, a well-known radio personality. After a warm handshake, Linkletter took Jack off to the Press Club. There they ran into a friend of Linkletter's, the advertising manager of the Roma Wine Company. He was greatly impressed on being introduced to a giant—especially one who had appeared before millions of circusgoers.

A shoe manufacturer in St. Louis had engaged the young giant Robert Wadlow, whom we met earlier, to travel across the country and publicize the company's products. Why, the sales manager wondered, shouldn't he get Jack to do the same thing for Roma wines? Then and there he hired him to make a three-month tour calling on Roma's customers as a goodwill ambassador.

Jack took to his new job like a fish to water. Roma's customers took to him too. The three months passed faster than any other three months in his life. He had to pinch himself when Roma told him they wanted him to work for them permanently as a salesman and promoter. His worries about his future were over.

Traveling for the wine company, Jack soon was making three or four trips across the United States every year. He was on the move now more than when he'd been with the circus—but he was really having fun for a change.

No longer was he just a freak standing motionless in front of nameless crowds. He was talking to customers face-to-face, winning friends and influencing people. The harder he worked, the more he earned. The wine merchants could never get over the novelty of having a giant call on them. Many wanted him to pose for photographs with them and their families.

Jack's tall figure and friendly smile quickly became well known to conductors on the railroads. He always traveled in a large compartment, and the porters soon learned how to make up a double berth for him. In the hotels where he stayed, maids were notified in advance to push two beds end to end.

The giant salesman had many amusing experiences. He never tired of telling the story of the girl elevator operator who stopped at a floor where he was waiting. When the door opened she couldn't see his lofty head; she thought a headless body was standing in front of her. In shock, she dropped the elevator four floors, screaming. After that, he said, he always stooped as the elevator door opened.

Jack would never forget what happened on his first day on the job. Roma had its headquarters in San Francisco, so he started his selling career there. By mistake he made a call at a small delicatessen. A short Italian woman was standing behind the counter when he entered, his hat scraping the ceiling. Eyes almost popping out of her head, she let out a shriek and ran into a back room.

A minute later a man came out, her husband. He was just as short and just as scared. But he balled his fists, ready to fight the intruder.

Jack was flustered. Reaching into his pocket, he pulled out his business card.

His hand trembling, the proprietor read it. "All right!" he cried. "I take one case anything you got, then you scram. Good-bye!"

Jack, who had been billed by the circus as the Tallest Man on Earth, now found Roma calling him "the Tallest Salesman in the World." In his new job his height was a big plus. "No secretary ever tells me her boss is in conference," he said. His customers never forgot his name.

As he moved up in the company, he was called upon to conduct sales meetings. Nobody's attention ever wandered when the giant was talking.

Jack made his home in San Francisco. The Palace Hotel, where he stayed when he was in town, kept an enormous room available for him, with a special bed, nine feet by six. When he went on the road his personal possessions were stored at the hotel. Among them were his fishing rods—they looked more like flagpoles—and his oversized shotgun. (He enjoyed target shooting.)

A big man needs a big chair. To show its appreciation of its talented new employee, Roma had a special chair constructed for his office. It was, he would swear, the only one he ever felt completely comfortable in.

Jack's car, which he drove when he called on the wine trade on the West Coast, was also pretty special. It was a large five-passenger coupe, and he had it altered to take his huge frame. The front seat was removed, and about twenty inches were added to the steering-wheel shaft; when driving, he sat on the backseat. He found the upper part of the steering wheel blocked his view, so he had this section removed. He liked to say that his car was probably the only expensive one in San Francisco without theft insurance—no one but another giant could drive it!

Earlier we saw that Jack couldn't find ready-made clothing in his size. Four times a year he would order a new suit from a tailor in Hollywood. The tailor kept a special pattern he'd made to the giant's measurements, so he didn't have to be measured again; all Jack had to do was select the material. It took eight yards of cloth to make a suit.

Buying socks for his enormous feet had to be done in quantity. The factory needed to do special tooling to make socks his size, and Jack had to order them a gross at a time. Everything else he wore was also made to order—suspenders, belts, eyeglasses, gloves, and hats, as well as the four-and-a-half-carat ring on his finger. (Luckily he had a jeweler in the family.)

Women are supposed to prefer tall men. But what if the man is a giant?

No accounts have come down to us of romantic attachments in Jack's case. But he was interested in the ladies, as a woman who knew him in El Paso, Rosemary Fryer, recalled recently. In 1940 Jack turned up at a New Year's Eve dance. She was dancing with her escort when Jack tapped him on the shoulder, and he yielded her to the giant.

"My hand was swallowed in Jake's enormous hand," she said. "As he guided me around the dance floor, I had a hard time keeping up with him because he took such big steps, so I placed my feet on top of his shoes and we danced all over. I was so embarrassed, my cheeks burned red and I felt that everyone was looking at us. I breathed a sigh of relief when Jack was tapped on the shoulder and he turned me over to a young man."

Pathological giants are usually quite shy, if not sexually underdeveloped; they seldom marry. On the other hand, quite a number of "normal" giants—exceptionally tall people who are the children of tall parents—have been married, sometimes to other giants. The most famous giant couple in history was Anna Swan and

Anna Swan, the Nova Scotia Giantess, with her husband, Captain Martin Bates, a former Confederate Army officer, are the tallest married couple on record.

Captain Martin Bates (she was seven feet five and one-half inches tall, he a few inches shorter). They built themselves a giant house in Seville, Ohio, and became the parents of a giant baby. The infant weighed an astonishing twenty-three and three-quarters pounds at birth, but unfortunately it didn't live.

If Jack didn't have children of his own, he certainly enjoyed spending time with other people's. Every year, at Christmas, he'd dress up in an extra-large Santa Claus costume and attach a white beard to his chin. Then the Tallest Santa Claus on Earth would head for orphanages or the pediatric wards of hospitals on the West Coast. There he entertained the children, telling them stories and singing carols in his fine clear voice. He also wrote a book for children.

In his postcircus career Jack's personality had blossomed. Instead of being withdrawn, he was now outgoing and friendly. He even took a course in public speaking, so he'd feel more at ease talking to groups. During World War II he made public appearances to raise money for the war effort, helping to sell thousands of dollars worth of war bonds.

His circle of friends widened as he made new acquaintances in business. He kept up with old ones too, like Harry Doll and his pretty sisters, whom he visited every winter at their home in Sarasota, where the circus had its winter quarters. He also visited his family in El Paso, and he made plans to retire there someday.

In his new life, Jack would say, he felt as if he'd been reborn. Still, although he came out of his shell more and more, he would always remain a sensitive person.

Art still meant much to him. But now, instead of painting pictures of the circus, he painted California's sunny beaches, its wave-swept, jagged rocks. Often he gave his paintings to friends.

Himself the subject of countless photographs, Jack had a natural interest in taking pictures. He became an expert photographer; some of his shots won prizes. His best pictures were of people—of faces that were strong and full of character, like his own.

The giant loved poetry, and he loved to write it too. Most of his poems were very serious, sometimes even brooding. That's not hard to understand, if we recall the physical problems he'd had and still had—not to mention the psychological ones.

"There are thoughts I had as a boy that I still haven't escaped," he told Dean Jennings, a writer, in 1950. "I remember the grown people laughing at me. But I don't expect the world to be made over just for me. If I had a chance now to become a man of average size I don't think I'd take it. And when I feel low, I can go to my room and lock the door, and I can read, or paint, or write."

Jack published a book of his poems. Just as he did in real life, he cast long shadows in his poetry; perhaps that's why he named the book *Long Shadows*. It was written in free verse—without rhyme or meter. Only a few of the poems recalled his days with the circus. Here is one that's more typical:

> *Shadowy mists*
> *Swirl and steal*
> *Down the cornices*
> *Of my mind.*
> *Quietly at first,*
> *Then faster and faster, into the deep hiding places*
> *Of my terror*
> *They penetrate.*
> *My steps quicken . . . And I flee in fear*
> *From the pursuing shadows.*

A traveling salesman has to be on the go in all kinds of weather. One wintry day in the late 1940s Jack was driving on an icy road in California. Suddenly his car went out of control in a wild skid. The big automobile flipped over. He remained wedged inside for hours. Later a road crew found him. He was extricated and rushed to a hospital.

Jack's back was severely wrenched. He was sent to the Mayo Clinic in Rochester, Minnesota, for treatment.

"I suppose it was quite an event when I showed up in Rochester," he said. "They had to put two diathermy tables together and use two examination booths. They had a staff meeting for me and a seminar with all the endocrinologists. If nothing else, the world will remember me as the greatest guinea pig the Mayo ever had." He had to go back to the clinic again and again for treatment.

In January 1952 Jack decided it was time to call it quits. He retired and went home to El Paso.

He began to have a house built. It was to be a home for a giant—the rooms would be nine feet high, the shower heads in the bathrooms eight feet above the floor, the rest in proportion. He ordered furniture suitable for a man who weighed 370 pounds and was seven feet six and one-half inches tall.

Jack was looking forward to years of comfortable retirement among his relatives and old friends. From now on, he would be just plain Jake Erlich—not the circus giant or the giant salesman Jack Earle.

He wouldn't enjoy his retirement long.

Jack had seemed perfectly well when he arrived home. In June, however, his kidneys failed. His life in danger, he was rushed to the Hotel Dieu Hospital.

Nothing the doctors did could help the ailing giant. Day by day he sank.

On July 17, as the day ended, so did his life.

No ordinary coffin could hold his great body. One made to Jack's measurements had to be ordered from Dallas. Eight pallbearers were needed to carry his body to the grave in the B'nai Zion Cemetery.

Jack was only forty-six years old. It hadn't been a long life, as lives are lived nowadays. But, as his doctor said, "He had already lived longer than [pathological] giants usually live"—more than twice as long as poor Robert Wadlow, for example, who died at twenty-two.

Jack Earle—or Jake Erlich—was gone. But if it's true, as some say, that we live as long as we are remembered, he would continue to live a long, long time—not only for the vast numbers of circus fans and the people he'd met in business, but for the thousands of sick or lonely West Coast children to whom he'd brought warmth and hearty good cheer at a time in their lives when they needed it most.

Right to the end—and beyond—Jack's height continued to be exaggerated. "The friendly giant," said the *Sarasota Herald-Tribune* in its obituary, "was eight feet seven inches tall."

Reading it, Jack would have smiled his giant smile, chuckled, and shaken his head.

Ishi
August 29, 1911

The Last "Wild" Indian
in North America

Oroville is a small country town in northern California, in the foothills of the Cascade Mountains. Its name means "gold town"—and that's what it became when gold was discovered there in 1848. Hordes of prospectors swooped down upon the region like flies upon honey, and they would not depart until they had dredged or washed out the last of the glittering metal. In 1911, when our story begins, its place had been taken by another kind of gold, shining groves of orange trees.

About three miles outside the town stood the Ward slaughterhouse. A team of men toiled inside in bloody overalls. Outside was a corral, on which hung the drying hides of butchered cattle. The smell of blood lingered in the air. Sturdy watchdogs patrolled the property.

One day in late August, as the twilight settled, the peace of the evening was splintered by the excited yipping of the guard dogs. The butchers grabbed their guns and rushed out the door.

In the gloom they made out a dark figure inside the corral. A circle of barking dogs surrounded it, their jaws slavering.

Only a single intruder—and unarmed. The butchers breathed more easily.

As they came closer, they saw it was an American Indian, an older one. He appeared more terrified of them and their weapons than he did of the dogs.

One of the butchers hurried inside to telephone the sheriff in Oroville. The rest stood around the man, their guns trained on him.

After a time they heard the rattle of wagon wheels and the clatter of hooves. A wagon pulled up, and they could see the tense faces of J. B. Webber, sheriff of Butte County, and his deputy.

Jumping down, the lawmen hurried toward the crouching figure of the Indian, guns at the ready.

They saw at a glance they would not need them. The man, his body covered to the knees by a long nightshirt-like garment of old canvas, was little more than skin and bones. He appeared close to collapse and half-frightened to death. A pair of handcuffs was snapped on his unresisting wrists.

Who are you? What are you doing here? The sheriff's questions produced only a blank stare from the native. They helped him into the wagon, and when they reached the county jail he was lodged in a cell.

In a small town like Oroville the taking of the strange Indian was a big event. Before long, townspeople began coming to the jail to get a look at the fellow—one thousand on the first day. They had seen many Indians, but never one who looked and behaved like this one. To the newspapers he quickly became "the Wild Man of Oroville." When people tried to talk to him they got no reply, not even when they spoke in Spanish, which many Native Americans understood.

The local Indians, just as curious about the newcomer, started dropping in. They spoke to him in their languages, Maidu and Wintun. He answered very politely—but in a language nobody had ever heard.

Sheriff Webber studied his prisoner. Prisoner? He couldn't properly be called one—he had done nothing wrong. Actually, the sheriff was keeping him in the cell mostly to protect him from the visitors. He would be kept there, this strange, sad-looking fellow, until Webber could find out what to do with him.

Could he be a Yahi, the sheriff wondered. A small tribe, the Yahi had once lived not far away, on Deer Creek. But white settlers kept moving in. The Yahi had been wiped out years ago—or so everybody said.

The Indian looked starved. He was offered food but refused to touch it. Perhaps he feared it had been poisoned. Years back, sometimes the whites had left poisoned food where the Indians would find it. Many had died.

As the hours passed, the Indian's hunger must have grown stronger than his fear. When a bowl of beans and some bread and butter were brought to him later, he began to gobble them down as fast as he could.

A sympathetic deputy held out a doughnut. Clutching the bowl of beans with one hand, the Indian accepted the doughnut and examined it curiously. He tried a cautious nibble. The instant he tasted it, the bowl was put down and he devoured the doughnut ravenously.

The Indian was soon to become acquainted with more of the white man's foods. The good ladies of Oroville, taking pity on him, brought things to eat to the jail. Bananas, oranges, apples, and other fruits— he looked at them as if he had never seen such things before.

He was given a banana. He began to cram it into his mouth, skin and all. They showed him that the fruit should be peeled first. He smacked his lips as he ate it.

He started to eat an orange, and again he had to be shown it must be peeled.

The lesson was learned at last—but it was learned too well. When he was given his first tomato, he began to peel it too.

The good ladies brought soup to him. He studied it a moment, and then he started to ladle it into his mouth with his fingers. A spoon was placed in his hand and he was shown what to do with it; this wonderful invention pleased him mightily. So did a knife and fork, and he quickly learned to use them.

Of all the white man's foods, none pleased him as much as ice cream and popcorn. He could never get enough of them.

As an experiment, the sheriff took the cartridges out of a six-shooter and placed it in the Indian's hands. He turned it this way and that, examining it with interest. It was clear he had never handled a gun before—although very likely he had looked into the business end of one in the past.

For the first time he saw someone writing on a piece of paper. He was spellbound. The squiggles on the sheet mystified him.

A plug of chewing tobacco was held out to him. He took a bite, but, not understanding it was to be chewed, he gulped it down and indicated he found it delightful.

Given a cigarette, he had no idea what was to be done with it, but it didn't take him long to learn. He was taught to roll his own—many people did so at the time—and soon the ends of his fingers were tobacco-stained.

To the "wild man," the white man's civilization appeared to be completely new. Probably he had come in touch with it only when he broke into some settler's cabin in the wilderness where he had made his home. The nightshirt he wore was doubtless loot from such a raid.

The *Oroville Register,* on August 29, was full of the story of the Indian's capture. The newspaper decided he might well be the last of "the Deer Creek tribe of wild and uncivilized Indians . . . probably today the wildest people in America." Picked up at once by the press in other cities in California, the story was wired across the country.

No one read the report of the "wild" Indian's discovery with greater excitement than two young anthropologists at the University of California in Berkeley.

Anthropology, the study of humankind, was a fairly new science in 1911. One of the two, Alfred Kroeber, was the university's first professor of anthropology. He and his colleague, T. T. Waterman, were devoted to the study of the Indians of California.

The state had once been home to many Native American tribes, but their numbers had shrunk with the coming of the white man. Thousands had been killed or driven from their lands, or had fallen victim to the white man's diseases. The two professors frequently visited what remained of the tribes; they wanted to learn everything they could about their languages and their vanishing way of life. That was an important part of their job as anthropologists.

Now, suddenly, here were these reports of a wild Indian—an aborigine—perhaps the last of the tribe, the Deer Creek Indians or Yahi, which everyone believed to be extinct. A genuine primitive, untouched by the white man and his ways!

On August 31 Sheriff Webber received a telegram. In it Kroeber said:

> NEWSPAPERS REPORT CAPTURE WILD INDIAN SPEAKING
> LANGUAGE OTHER TRIBES TOTALLY UNABLE UNDERSTAND.
> PLEASE CONFIRM OR DENY BY COLLECT TELEGRAM AND
> IF STORY CORRECT HOLD INDIAN TILL ARRIVAL
> PROFESSOR STATE UNIVERSITY WHO WILL TAKE CHARGE
> AND BE RESPONSIBLE FOR HIM. MATTER IMPORTANT
> ACCOUNT ABORIGINAL HISTORY.

Sheriff Webber replied he would do so, and Waterman hurried to get the train to Oroville.

Young Professor Waterman peered with rising excitement at the Indian sitting on the cot in the cell.

He was still dressed in the rough nightshirt-like garment, and his feet were bare—well-shaped, natural feet that had never known shoes. He must be about fifty years old, Waterman thought. When the Indian stood up he was perhaps five feet eight inches tall. His eyes were large and black, his nose wide, his mouth large. His reddish bronze or coppery skin was lighter than that of most Native Americans—and the Deer Creek tribe was said to have skin like that.

The Indian's hair, thick and jet black, was very short. The professor understood at once that the man had burned it off; some Indians did that when they mourned a dead relative. The lobes of his ears were pierced, and from them hung knotted strings of animal sinew. The septum of his nose had also been pierced to hold a plug of wood. These objects were "medicine"—religious talismans that assured he would go to heaven when he died.

The Indian stirred uneasily. Waterman, smiling, spoke to him in English; his tone was gentle and reassuring. Then, sitting down beside him, he pulled out a sheet of paper. It contained a list of words in Yana, a language related to Yahi. Would the man understand them?

One by one, Waterman read the words aloud, pronouncing them with care. The Indian was all attention, but his grave, sensitive face gave no sign he recognized any of them. As Waterman worked his way down the list, he began to lose hope.

He came to the word *siwin,* which means yellow pine. As he pronounced it, he tapped the pine wood of the cot. The Indian's face lit up; he nodded in vigorous agreement.

Waterman repeated the word. The Indian said it too, but he pronounced it in a different way. Both men tapped the cot joyfully.

Waterman continued reading, finding more words the Indian recognized. The anthropologist smiled happily. This man had to be a member of the Deer Creek tribe!

Warming to each other, the two men were soon saying things, the Indian in Yahi, Waterman in Yana, his eyes jumping up and down the list. Then, surprisingly, the Indian said: *"I ne ma Yahi?"* ("Are you a Yahi?")

Waterman answered that he was.

Of course the Indian could see he wasn't—not this man with the white skin, the mustache, the glasses. Suddenly, however, the Indian's whole manner had become easier, more relaxed.

In this place of strangers he had found a friend.

"It was a pleasure to see him open his eyes when he heard Yana from me," wrote Waterman to Kroeber. "And he looked over my shoulder at the paper [the list of words] in a most mystified way. He knew at once where I got my inspiration. . . . We showed him some arrows last night, and we could hardly get them away from him. He showed us how he flaked the points, singed the edges of the feathers, and put on the sinew wrappings."

If only the Yahi could talk—*really* talk—to him!

A deputy was sent to bring an Indian who might help. This was Batwi, an elderly member of the Northern Yana, a tribe related to the Yahi. Batwi had provided the anthropologists with the word list Waterman was using. Batwi spoke English, and through him Waterman should be able to communicate with the Yahi.

When Batwi came, he greeted the "wild Indian" in Northern Yana. The Yahi drew back in alarm. His tribe and Batwi's had been deadly enemies for generations.

But Batwi looked anything but threatening. He had a gray beard, he wore glasses, he dressed like a white man, and he was smiling. His appearance quickly reassured the Yahi. Although their languages were different, they were not entirely so; the two Indians could understand each other more or less.

Meanwhile, telegrams were flying back and forth between Kroeber in Berkeley and the Bureau of Indian Affairs in Washington, D.C. The bureau was responsible for the welfare of Native Americans, and it granted permission for the Yahi to be brought to the university, where the staff would take charge of him for the present. A final decision would be made later.

On September 4—just six days after the Yahi had been discovered—Waterman set out with him on the journey south. Batwi went along as interpreter. The Yahi, for most of his life, had lived inside a small area, only forty by sixty miles square. The trip ahead would be 180 miles—the longest journey he had made in his life.

During his short stay in the county jail the Yahi had put on weight. For his trip, the townspeople had provided him with appropriate clothing, including a new suit. They had also given him a pair of shoes. But he had never worn anything like them in his life, and he absolutely refused to put them on. Instead, he carried them with him, one in each hand.

At the railroad station a crowd was waiting to bid the departing guest farewell. A quick learner, he smiled as one of the ladies took his picture. His smile was tense, but still it was a smile.

Train number 5, blowing its whistle and trailing clouds of smoke, chugged toward the station. The sound was not new to the Yahi—

the train had passed daily not far from his tribe's hiding places. In the past, when he heard it, he had always lain down to hide in the grass or the brush; to him it was a strange and fearsome monster. The sight of the smoking iron beast so close at hand filled him with terror. He ran and hid behind a cottonwood tree.

Waterman had told him that he had nothing to fear from the noisy, evil-smelling monster, and he speedily realized that was true. Rejoining Batwi and Waterman, he climbed aboard and allowed himself to be guided to a seat.

All through the long journey the Yahi's handsome features remained expressionless. If you

Ishi (right), soon after his arrival, with Batwi and Professor Kroeber.

had looked closely, however, you might have noticed a tension about his mouth; his eyes had narrowed and his fists were clenched. But of what he felt as he traveled in the belly of the monster he said nothing.

The train ride came to an end in Oakland, on San Francisco Bay. At the quay a ferry was waiting to carry them across the water.

On the other side, a startling experience lay in store for the Indian—his first trolley car ride, up to Parnassus Heights, where the university's Museum of Anthropology stood. Jolting along on the trolley, with its clanging bell and its sudden stops and starts, this man from the deep silences of Deer Creek must have felt he was living in a nightmare.

The next day Batwi was asked how the Yahi had reacted to the trip. Batwi chuckled. "First, yesterday, he frightened very much, now today he think all very funny. He like it, tickle him. He like this place here. Much to see, big water off there . . . plenty houses, many things to see."

The university proper was in Berkeley, across the bay, but its brand-new Museum of Anthropology was in San Francisco, above Golden Gate Park. In the museum, as yet unopened, would be displayed the huge and varied collection the university had been gathering for years, telling the story of peoples around the world, not least of all the Indians of California.

The small maintenance staff lived in the building. There was also a room where visiting Indians stayed from time to time, while the anthropologists interviewed them and studied their languages. This room, from now on, would be the Yahi's home.

That first night, at bedtime, the new resident brought smiles to the faces of Waterman and Batwi. He was unwilling to take off his clothes. He had never seen white men without their clothing, he said—and so he was going to keep his on too.

Next morning the Yahi met Alfred Kroeber for the first time. A handsome, bearded, friendly man of thirty-five, Kroeber was both the curator of the museum and the head of the Department of Anthropology; he knew more about the life and languages of the Indians of California than almost anyone. He and the Yahi took to each other at once. The Indian could see that Kroeber was in charge, and from that day he would refer to him as the "Chiep." (The Yahi couldn't pronounce the sound f.)

The Last "Wild" Indian in North America

For the newcomer, it was to be one of the most remarkable days of his life. His eyes were wide with astonishment when he was led through the museum's Native American collection. Waterman was busy with pen and pad as the Yahi gave, in his language, the names of hundreds of the objects. Batwi interpreted, with the superior, self-important air of one who knew it all.

The Yahi was shown some things found a few years earlier in an abandoned Yahi camp. He began to talk a blue streak. Some belonged to him, he said; he had been obliged to run off and leave them when white men—*saldu* was the Yahi word he used for them—appeared out of nowhere.

Waterman was as eager to teach the Yahi about the new world he had stumbled into as he was to learn from him. During a telephone call, he put the receiver to the Indian's ear. A look of dismay spread across the bronze face. The powers of the *saldu* were awesome!

To Kroeber and Waterman, as to all who met the Yahi, there was something simple and charming about him. He was like a child, with all of a child's wonder about new things. Given a whistle and shown how to blow it, he couldn't get over the sound it made. This treasure he kept in his pocket—pockets were another discovery, and they were rapidly filled with precious new possessions. Taking the whistle out from time to time, he blew it loudly, laughing with all the delight of a four-year-old.

The arrival of the aborigine in San Francisco was a major news event, and that afternoon a crowd of reporters and photographers came bustling up to the museum. The Yahi was wearing a blue shirt and overalls when he was introduced. They wanted to photograph him, but they protested it just wouldn't do to show the last of the Yahi in white man's clothing. So a garment made of animal skins was hunted up in the museum's collection and he was asked to put it on.

Always good-natured and eager to please, now he suddenly refused.

He would not take off his white man's clothing for anyone.

It was a repeat of the bedtime incident.

"He say," reported the interpreter, "he not see other people go without them, and he say he never take them off no more."

But the Yahi's wish to make his new friends happy won out. The skins were draped over him, and the overall legs were rolled up so they wouldn't show. He stood with a half smile on his face as six cameras clicked, but his taut mouth showed he was far from happy.

Otherwise, though, the Indian appeared to be having the time of his life. The newsmen found him highly likable—an intelligent person with a delightful sense of humor.

What was the Yahi's name, the reporters wanted to know.

Batwi put the question to him. He got no answer.

To Kroeber and Waterman, that came as no surprise. Aborigines around the world will not tell outsiders their real name. They fear that if it becomes known to an enemy, he can make "bad medicine"—put a jinx on them. Among Native Americans it was considered bad etiquette even to ask it. Usually they were called by nicknames.

"We can't go on calling him 'Hey there,'" said Waterman.

Kroeber nodded. The word *ishi*, in Yahi, means man; that, Kroeber suggested, would be a suitable name—and, from that moment on, the Indian was Ishi to everybody. He made no objection.

A bow and arrow from the museum were placed in Ishi's hands. A cameraman, taking off his new felt hat, placed it on a stick about a hundred feet away. In sign language Ishi was asked to shoot at it. It was all intended as a joke; its owner believed the hat was in no danger.

Everyone laughed, and the Indian joined in. He fitted the arrow to the bowstring, sighted it, released it, and it went whistling through the air. He danced with glee as it ripped through the hat, to the photographer's dismay.

Ishi was given a pair of fire sticks. No one present had ever seen an Indian use them. One was a flattened little slab of soft wood with a hole in it; the other, the drill, was a straight, slender stick. Squatting down with the ends of the slab under the toes of each foot, he placed one end of the drill in the hole and began to twirl it rapidly between his palms, first left, then right, pressing down hard. A small pile of wood dust began to accumulate on the wood slab. Soon it started to smoke and a spark appeared; he nursed it until he had set the wood dust on fire. The newsmen applauded.

Ishi, caught up in the spirit of the occasion, was showing off like a young boy. Placing a leaf between his lips, he sucked strongly on it, and a sound was heard like the bleating of a young fawn. This was one of the ways he had lured deer when hunting. He pantomimed drawing back a bowstring. He squatted down and made a delicate sound, with a make-believe bow and arrow at the ready; this was how he lured rabbits.

How did he hunt bear? He laughed and pantomimed climbing up a tree.

The reporters had found a wonderful story in Ishi, and the newspapers were full of him. Big-money offers came flooding in to the university almost at once. Theaters, showmen, the circus—all wanted to sign up the Yahi. They offered to include Kroeber in the act.

Nothing doing, said the anthropologist.

"In Ishi," declared Professor Kroeber, "we have the most uncivilized and uncontaminated man in the world today." Ishi, he went on, was the last of his tribe; when he died, its language, its beliefs, its ancient ways would be lost forever. Some of the skills he possessed, like using the fire drill and making arrow points of flint, went back to the Stone Age, to the days of the caveman. He could teach us how our ancestors lived forty thousand years ago.

Ishi was a priceless living document. The university did not intend to lend him to anybody.

■ ■ ■

Many small Indian nations, or tribes, lived in California before the coming of the white man. Like nations today, sometimes they lived in peace, and sometimes there was war between them.

There were four different tribes of Yana—the Northern, Central, and Southern Yana, and the Yahi Yana—living in north central California. Made up of small bands, each tribe had its own territory. Their customs were similar, but each spoke a different dialect of the same language. All told, they did not number more than a few thousand.

The Yahi lived in the southernmost part of the range, in the foothills of the Cascade Mountains. It was a rugged land, creased with deep canyons and covered with dense brush, called chaparral, and trees. The canyons had been hollowed out by streams over thousands of years. Deer Creek and Mill Creek were the best known. Above towered Mount Lassen, 10,465 feet high, with its snow-covered peak. The Indians called the mountain Waganupu.

The Yahi built their villages along the green-covered banks of the creeks or on the ledges of the cliffs above. They had not discovered how to plant and grow crops, as the Indians did elsewhere, but were hunters and gatherers. The men speared salmon in the streams or hunted deer, elk, rabbits, antelopes, or bears. The women gathered bulbs, roots, greens, berries, and, especially, acorns, which they used to pound and make into a mush, their principal food. They also wove baskets, and these they used to boil food in or to store it. To make clothing and blankets, they sewed animal skins together.

Like the other Yana tribes, the Yahi lived this way for thousands of years. According to Kroeber, the Yana were probably the oldest group of Indians living in California.

In 1848 the quiet world of the Indians of northern California was turned upside down when gold was discovered. Prospectors poured in by the thousands. Many came by the Lassen Trail, a route that cut through the land of the Yahi.

A large number of the new arrivals, along with their other baggage, brought a fierce hatred of Indians.

Conflict between the Native Americans and the invading whites was as old as the first settlements in America. "A good Indian is a dead Indian" was a widely held belief. Prospectors might shoot down a Yana the instant they saw one. They raided the Indian villages, massacred the inhabitants, and took their scalps.* Sometimes women and children would be carried off and sold as slaves. Settlers seized the Indian lands and claimed them as their own.

Occasionally this dark story had a bright side. In some places the settlers lived in peace with their Native American neighbors. They needed household help and workers to assist in tilling the soil of their homesteads or caring for their livestock, and they hired Yana to work for them. Some of these Indians were highly thought of and treated as members of the family.

But such cases were the exception, not the rule. To avoid death or capture, the Yana had to abandon places where they had lived for generations and run for their lives. They took refuge in remote areas—places where the undergrowth was so dense or the terrain so rough the white man stayed away.

Not all the Indians gave up easily. Often the Yana put up stiff resis-

---

*Scalping was unknown to the California Indians before the arrival of the whites. Some counties promoted it by offering fifty cents for each scalp brought in; five dollars was paid for each head. An account of scalping and the warfare with the Indians may be found in the author's book *Captured by the Indians* (Dover, 1985) and the audiocassette version *Journals of the Pioneers* (Recorded Books, 1981).

tance—stiffer, we are told, than any of the other tribes of the Pacific Coast. Sometimes, when they could, they struck back, making raids upon the white settlements. But, in the long run, they could do little to stop the advance of the invaders.

In August 1864 several Indians, described as "outlaws," murdered two white women and injured their children.

The region was full of prospectors, men who hungered for excitement. They organized attacks on the Yana villages, shooting down men, women, and children without mercy. They even invaded the homesteads of settlers who lived on good terms with the Yana and murdered any who were there, stealing the money they found in their pockets.

Here's a typical incident, one of many. Some miners came uninvited into the home of a white woman, where they discovered a seven-year-old Yana girl. Ignoring the woman's protests, they seized the child and shot her dead.

"We must kill them, big and little," their leader told the woman. "Nits will be lice."

That year most of the remaining Yana were killed. As many as two thousand are estimated to have lost their lives. Today we would call what was done there genocide.

By 1870 no more than a few dozen of the Northern and Central Yana remained alive. The Southern Yana had been wiped out. So too, it was said, had all of the Yahi.

In the deep canyon fastnesses, however, a handful of Yahi still held on. One of these, many years later, would be named Ishi.

Ishi was born in about 1862, in a village on Deer Creek. When he was only a small child the villagers were compelled to flee for their lives. They found another place to live, one that seemed safer, close to a stream and hidden by tall oak trees, where they could harvest the acorns that were so precious to them. Here, once more, they built their homes, dome-shaped huts made with poles, which they covered with thatch and mud, just as they had for generations.

On August 16, 1865—Ishi was about three—a volley of shots rang out in the early morning. He and his mother and father scrambled out of their hut and ran for their lives.

The shooting continued. Many tried to escape by throwing themselves into the creek. But the attackers had been prepared for that; the creek ran scarlet with Yahi blood.

More than forty Indians lost their lives that day. The boy would never see his father again.

The little family, with the few remaining members of their band, set up new huts on the bank of Mill Creek. Food was scarcer than ever. The deer and other game were disappearing as the settlers shot them and cut down the forests. Fish were harder to find in streams polluted with mining debris.

Still, the Yahi followed the ancient ways. At a harvest festival, all who were left came. Young Ishi counted the number of people at the celebration. About forty.

It was the most people he would see for thirty years.

Every year the tribe kept shrinking. Its members drew back further and further into the shelter of the dense woodland.

Fires had to be tended with greater care than ever, so the *saldu* would not see flames or smoke. The Yahi no longer dared to fish or hunt in broad daylight. To avoid leaving footprints, they leaped from stone to stone; they walked in the streams rather than on their banks; they trod in the trails of the deer and antelope, and if their bare feet left marks they brushed them away or spread leaves over them. Once the hunters, they had become the hunted.

Ishi reached manhood. He could not marry; there was no woman left for him to marry. Driven by hunger, he sometimes broke into cabins in the woods when their white owners were away. His sister and a few others went with him. Once they stole some clothing from a cabin, but, just as they were leaving, they found themselves face-to-face with a *saldu*. They expected to be killed, but the man took pity on them and let them keep what they had taken.

A few months later, the man, returning to his cabin, found two lovely Yahi baskets inside. It was the Indians' way of saying thanks.

The search for safety was unending. Finally Ishi found a cave on a ledge in the canyon wall, about five hundred feet up from Deer Creek and two hundred below the canyon rim. It had once been the den of a bear; the Indians called it Wowunupo, the Grizzly Bear's Hiding Place. Here Ishi settled with his mother and sister, and two men who had joined their family.

For more living space they built a small room at the mouth of the cave and roofed it with thatch and earth. They also built a smokehouse and a cookhouse, a rack for drying salmon and deer meat, and huts to live in when the weather turned warm. Ishi would follow an old bear's trail down the side of the canyon to reach the creek and the woods below. On the ledge the Yahi felt secure, for their dwelling place was screened by trees.

In this lonely setting the five Indians lived for years. In time one of the men died and the other grew very old. Ishi's mother grew old too; she had a stroke and was partly paralyzed.

Time drew lines in the faces of Ishi and his sister. As Native

Americans had always done, they took good care of the two old people, providing them with food and seeing they were warm in winter.

In November 1908, once again white men drew close to the hiding place of the Yahi. They were surveyors, working for the Oro Power and Light Company, which was planning to build a dam on the creek.

At dusk one day Ishi was standing in the creek, harpoon in hand, watching for a fish to spear. He glanced about, as he always did in these dangerous times. Not far off he saw two *saldu* watching him. He shook his harpoon angrily and cried out. The men disappeared into the bushes.

Afraid he might be followed, Ishi waited a long time before he dared to go back home. When he finally reached the cave, he told the others what had happened. That night he was afraid to light a fire or even sleep.

Next day, armed with his bow and arrows, he headed down the bear's trail. All at once he beheld a *saldu* coming toward him. He fired an arrow instantly. As he did so, the man turned and fled.

Ishi hurried back up to the ledge. We must leave here quickly, very quickly, he told his little band.

They were gathering up their belongings when they heard loud noises close by.

Take the old man and go this minute, Ishi ordered his sister.

He looked at his poor old mother. She was unable to move; how could he carry her and get away in time? The best he could do was throw a blanket over her and hope she would not be discovered. Then he took to his heels.

Ishi had just reached the safety of the woods when the whites appeared at the cave entrance. Drawing back the blanket, they found the feeble old woman. After giving her some water, they gathered up everything movable. Not only the Indians' provisions, but their baskets, clothing, weapons, tools, and blankets, which made splendid souvenirs for the *saldu*. For the Yahi, the loss of these precious objects would mean terrible hardship in the winter—if not death.

After a while Ishi crept back. At any time the whites might reappear. Lifting the helpless woman, he bore her away to safety.

But now another worry hammered at him. Where were his sister and the old man? Moving about cautiously, he searched for them high and low. Bears and cougars still roamed the region. The two missing people could have fallen prey to them. Or perhaps they had tried to swim across the creek and drowned. Nowhere could he find any trace of them.

As his people had done for ages, he sang the death chant for them; he burned his hair short in mourning, and prayed they would find the trail to the Land of the Dead. But he had been unable to burn their bodies, as his religion required, and he was afraid their unhappy souls might be condemned to wander the earth forever.

In the last years, life had not been easy for Ishi—but now his world was falling apart completely. Not long after the flight from the ledge, his mother closed her eyes, never to open them again. For the first time he discovered the true meaning of loneliness. Everyone he had known and loved was gone. All of the Yahi, except for himself, had vanished from the face of the earth. No one was left he could talk to, laugh with, cry with. He was completely and utterly alone.

Native Americans were used to isolation and hardship. But they had good times too. For the last of the Yahi, it seemed good times could never come again.

For the next three years Ishi lived by himself. The wilderness surrounding Waganupu—Mount Lassen—kept shrinking. Life had lost its meaning, and the loneliness became unbearable.

Finally, exhausted, starving, grieving for his loved ones, he wandered away. Mile after mile he walked aimlessly, his mind clouded, until he came out of the woods and beheld the corral in front of the slaughterhouse outside Oroville. Climbing over the fence, he lay down under a great oak tree that grew there. He did not care whether he lived or died.

Kroeber and Waterman could hardly believe their great good fortune. A genuine aborigine had never come their way before. Ishi could unlock priceless treasures of knowledge about America's earliest inhabitants—people of the Stone Age. From the very first day after his arrival at the museum, they busied themselves learning all they could from him.

Recordings of Ishi speaking his native language could be of great value to the science of anthropology. CDs and audiocassettes were still generations away, but thanks to the genius of Thomas Edison, voices could be recorded on wax cylinders.

A recording of Enrico Caruso, a famous opera star, was played for Ishi, and he was thrilled by the rich, powerful tones. Then he was seated in front of a recording machine and invited to speak into it. He looked at this strange device in puzzlement. But he was eager to oblige, and so his voice and the language of his people, its legends and songs, were set down on cylinder after cylinder over time—four hundred in all.

When the first cylinder was played back to Ishi, he listened in amazement. How had the machine learned to speak Yahi so fast? You can hear him today, his voice transferred to tape, if you ever visit the university's Phoebe Hearst Museum of Anthropology, now located in Berkeley.*

---

*More than sixty songs sung by Ishi were recorded. They include a thunder song, a flint song, a fish song, a shaman's bow song, a foot song, a girl's song, a shaman's song against rattlesnake bite, and a good number of gambling songs.

A picture record of the vanished way of life of the Yahi would be invaluable. At Kroeber's bidding, Ishi did many of the things he had done in the wilderness, while a camera clicked away—things very commonplace to him but fascinating to the anthropologists, who were seeing them for the first time.

Photographs could only show so much; for the whole story, moving pictures would be needed. The movie camera was new in that day, but it was used to capture Ishi in action. Unselfconsciously he showed how he used a fire drill to produce a flame. As the camera whirred, he showed how he made an arrowhead, breaking off a piece from a block of obsidian and chipping and finishing it. He demonstrated how he constructed a bow, strung it, and released the arrow. He trimmed his hair by burning it; he inserted in his nose an ornament made of shell; he spoke his language while close-ups were shot to show how he moved his lips.*

Early in Ishi's stay at the museum, Kroeber took him out for a drive through Golden Gate Park. The car came to a stop on a bluff overlooking Ocean Beach, and the two men looked down upon thousands of people enjoying the sunshine.

Oddly, the first thing Ishi commented on wasn't the great expanse of the ocean stretching before him.

"Hansi saldu!" ("So many white people!") he exclaimed to himself in a tone of disbelief. He repeated it over and over again. In his little world in the woods, he had never imagined there could be so many people on earth.

On their way back to the museum, the car startled a flock of quail on a little-traveled street, and they rose in flight. Ishi looked surprised

---

*Unfortunately, little was known about the proper storage and preservation of film in those early days, and the movies of Ishi deteriorated completely.

and tremendously pleased—as if, Kroeber thought, he was seeing old friends.

As the car drove on, Ishi turned to watch the flying birds.

"Chickakatee!" he called to them in a gentle voice. *"Chickakatee!"*

Ishi, who had feared the *saldu* all his life, was soon on friendly terms with everyone at the museum. But his fear of whites was ingrained, and strangers still frightened him. When five or six people he didn't know came close, a troubled look would darken his face, and his hands would grow rigid. He didn't like to be touched by a white person. Over time, however, he learned to shake hands when he was introduced to somebody.

Not long after Ishi's arrival, the official opening of the new museum

In the theater with Batwi and Kroeber. The Yahi liked the show,
but he was more impressed by the big audience.

was to take place. At a reception before the opening, close to a thousand special guests were to attend. Many, Kroeber knew, would want to meet his star, Ishi. How could he prepare him for the crowds? Kroeber told him it would be like an Indian housewarming. After that, Ishi could hardly wait for the day of the big event.

For the occasion, Ishi was dressed faultlessly—faultlessly, that is, with one exception: he still refused to wear shoes. (He would begin to wear them, however, when winter came.) It only took a single demonstration for him to learn how to tie his tie. The enormous crowd didn't fluster him; he simply remained on the outskirts, looking on with great curiosity.

Later, Kroeber asked Ishi to stay in a small exhibition room, and from time to time he brought in guests who had asked to meet him. Ishi was gracious and polite with everyone. He was, as employees at the museum always said, "a gentleman."

People all over the Bay Area had read about the "wild Indian" in the newspapers, and many wanted to see him for themselves. Kroeber announced in the press that Ishi and he would receive visitors on Sunday afternoons at the museum.

Sizable crowds turned up. Kroeber introduced Ishi to the audience and then took questions from them, translating for Ishi. His replies were thoughtful and intelligent. ("Ishi," Kroeber said, "has as good a head as any American.")

The Yahi gave demonstrations for the visitors, showing how he made an arrowhead, used his fire drill, and strung his bow. He would give away the finished arrowheads to members of the audience. After a while these finely made objects were in great demand—he made and distributed thousands. His Sunday performances were a great success; as many as a thousand people attended. Ishi took as much pleasure in them as any of the visitors. Over the years he received several marriage proposals, but declined them.

Except for the hours he worked with Kroeber and Waterman, teaching them Yahi and telling them about the ways of his people, the Indian was free to do as he pleased. He became a regular guest at Waterman's house, where he was a particular favorite of Mrs. Waterman and the children.

Before meals, he always washed his hands, which impressed them. At the table he watched Mrs. Waterman very closely, copying carefully the way she helped herself to food, held her fork, used her knife, or wiped her lips—and he did it all so rapidly that the two seemed to be acting in unison. She was so struck by his neatness that she hinted it wouldn't hurt Waterman to follow his example.

By November everyone at the museum regarded Ishi as a permanent fixture. He took his breakfast or lunch in the kitchen, cooking on a gas stove. For dinner, Kroeber and Waterman would take him to a restaurant or to their homes, or he would dine at a boardinghouse nearby. Out of their pockets they gave him money for tobacco, ice cream, or the movies, which he loved.

But the Indian had other needs, and some permanent arrangement would have to be made to satisfy them. To solve this problem, Kroeber had him placed on the university payroll as a "museum helper," at a salary of twenty-five dollars a month—much more money in that day than it is in this.

Nothing could have made Ishi happier. He had seen that white people had jobs and got paid and supported themselves. His spirit was an independent one; he hated to have to ask Waterman or Kroeber for money when he wanted something. He had already formed the habit of lending a helping hand to the janitor or the museum people when they were setting up exhibits. He liked having regular tasks to fill his free time, and it made him feel that he belonged. Because of the care and thoroughness with which he worked, Ishi was a valued helper. He did his job with, in Kroeber's words, "the same willing gentleness that marked all his actions."

The university's employees were paid by check. How would Ishi, who didn't know how to write, manage to endorse his? Kroeber wrote the Indian's name as simply as he could; then he gave him tracing paper to lay over it, and a pencil, and showed him how to trace it. Day after day Ishi practiced, until he could write it by himself.

John

Ishi's eyes shone with pleasure when his first check was placed in his hands. Laboriously he wrote his name on the back, and then rushed off with the precious piece of paper to a shop nearby, where he was known. As previously arranged, the owner gave him twenty-five silver dollars.

Before long Ishi was well known to the tradesmen on the block of shops near the museum. They called him by name and enjoyed talking to him. He spoke to them in a kind of pidgin English, a blend of English and Yahi, helped out with gestures. From the shopkeepers he bought tobacco, bread, groceries, and other things. When he saw something new—brightly colored objects particularly attracted him—he would ask, "How much money-tee?"*

For food Ishi liked beef and fish and all fruits and vegetables.

---

*In Yahi, -*tee* added to a word meant "is it?" or "it is."

Canned foods, like sardines and salmon, pleased him too. He was especially attached to ice-cream sodas; honey, candy, and jelly were other favorites. Bread he always ate without butter. He liked coffee and tea, but milk was not for him.

Before coming to the museum, Ishi had never tasted alcohol. Soon after his arrival, some people tried to get him drunk. That experience he never forgot; when someone asked him how he felt about drink, he said whiskey would make a man crazy and kill him.

Once he bought a few bottles of beer and drank small amounts after mixing it with sugar and water; he called it medicine. He much preferred ice-cream sodas.

The professors wanted to teach him English, but he showed a distinct unwillingness to learn it. He quickly picked up a number of common words, however—eventually as many as five or six hundred—enough for his everyday needs and interests. At the start he was self-conscious when he tried to speak the language of the *saldu*. "When he slips out a new English word or phrase," said Kroeber, "he blushes and smiles like a girl."

Certain sounds he could not make because they didn't exist in Yahi. One was *r*—he changed it to *l*, like the Chinese. A favorite phrase of his was: "Evelybody hoppy?" He said "good-boy" for "good-bye," but usually he preferred to say, "You stay—I go," or "You go?"

Although everybody was impressed by his politeness, he never learned to say "Thank you." If he was pleased with something you did for him, he would smile. If you gave him a present that he liked, he would say, "Him's good!"

He picked up quite a number of colloquial or slang phrases, especially from young boys. (He was particularly fond of them.) One day a visitor, a woman, asked him if he believed in God. "Sure, Mike!" he replied.

Although he never learned to read, he could recognize the commonest words on signs. He enjoyed looking at the comics, and sometimes he would laugh out loud at them.

Ishi loved to go places on the trolley. The sound of the gong pleased him enormously. He was able to identify the different trolleys by their numbers. He often made the combined trolley and ferry ride from the museum to the university in Berkeley across the bay and back. Sometimes he would stand for hours watching trolley cars go by.

The Yahi had been given a watch and chain which he wore with pride. Although he wound the watch regularly, he never set it, and he didn't consult it to tell the time. Instead, he relied on the position of the sun in the heavens for the approximate time, and he had some understanding of the clocks in the museum.

As with other Indians, Ishi's religion was an important part of his life. His ideas about what happens after death were those of his tribe, but he seemed to understand what Christianity was about. He asked many questions about heaven. Ishi doubted that the white God cared much about having Indians with Him, and he seemed to feel that women should not be allowed inside the Pearly Gates.

Once he saw a movie about Jesus. It affected him deeply. But he misunderstood the crucifixion, and supposed Jesus was a "bad man."

The Indian was appreciated by the university people not just for the knowledge he shared with them but for his friendly, likable personality. His reactions to modern customs and objects provided them with endless amusement. In the beginning, he was delighted whenever he turned on a faucet: imagine getting water by just turning something, instead of having to make the long trek down to the creek! Matches were a perpetual wonder to a man who all his life had been obliged to use a fire drill to produce a flame.

According to Waterman, Ishi was thrown for a loop the first time he encountered a window shade.

"On the morning of his second day at the museum," said Waterman, "I found him trying to raise the shade to let the sunlight in. It gave me a queer feeling to realize that never in his experience . . . had he encountered the common roller shade. He tried to push it to one side and it would not go. He pushed it up and it would not stay. I showed him how to give it a little jerk and let it run up. The subsequent five minutes he utilized for reflection. When I came back at the end of that time, he was still trying to figure out where the shade had gone."

Ishi was beardless when discovered, and he continued to be, yet he never used a razor. It was months before Kroeber observed how he kept his face so smooth: he pulled the hairs out as soon as they appeared, but always in private.

He was the soul of modesty. When he changed clothes and another person was present, he was always careful to cover his genitals. He shared his room with another employee, and wouldn't undress until the light was turned off.

Although he admitted that in years gone by he had stolen things from the cabins of *saldu* in the woods, the museum people found him unfailingly honest. He treated the possessions of others with as much respect as he expected them to treat his own. Once he saw his friend Waterman pick up and use a pencil that belonged to someone else, and he scolded him soundly.

Ishi had been in San Francisco only a few weeks when he began to sniffle. He had caught what we call the common cold—an ailment unknown to American aborigines until the white man introduced it. Later in his first year he would catch pneumonia, another illness brought to North America by the *saldu*. Without immunity to the white man's diseases, the lives of thousands and thousands of Native Americans were cut short. In the end, Ishi's would be too.

From Waterman's first day in Oroville, he and Ishi had an extremely close relationship. Only half the Indian's age, Waterman was enthusiastic and warmhearted, qualities that endeared him to Ishi. The Indian's name for him was "Watamany."

Kroeber, nine years older than Waterman, was already making a name for himself as one of America's foremost Indian experts. The head of both the museum and the anthropology department, he was a man of wisdom, with strong intellectual drive and ambition. To him Ishi was always a very special person, his ward and friend. When Kroeber went off on trips, he would send the Yahi picture postcards and small gifts that filled him with joy.

A third good friend of Ishi's was Dr. Saxton Pope. (Ishi's name for him was "Popey.") The university's hospital and medical school stood next to the museum, and Pope had first met the Indian when he came in for treatment.

One day, looking out of the window at the back of the building, Pope saw Ishi making a bow. Archery was a passion of the doctor's—he was himself a marksman with the English longbow—and what Ishi was doing fascinated him. He went out at once, and Ishi, fired by his enthusiasm, began to teach him the Yahi way of shooting.

"Ishi loved his bow as he loved nothing else in his possession," Pope said later. The two would pass many happy hours in each other's company, shooting with Pope's English bows, as well as with bows that Ishi made and bows from the museum. When Ishi saw how good Pope was with the bow he asked if he was part Indian. Unwilling to disappoint him, Pope said he was.

The doctor had another hobby: amateur magic. He had taught himself sleight-of-hand tricks to entertain his children, and he showed some of them to Ishi. After that, the Indian looked upon him with awe. Much more impressed by his skill as a magician than as a surgeon, Ishi thought of Pope as a *kuwi*, gifted with supernatural powers.*

Sometimes Popey would allow Ishi to sit in the surgical theater and watch an operation. The use of anesthesia amazed him. Once he observed Pope removing a diseased kidney from a patient; his eyes were fastened on the sleeping man in deep wonder. For days after, he kept asking Pope if the man was still alive, and found it hard to believe when the doctor said he was. When Ishi learned that the man was well enough to leave the hospital he was astonished.

Ishi had many other friends. One particularly good one was Edward Gifford, the assistant curator, whom he often helped in the museum. Another was Gifford's wife. She used to go on nature walks with Ishi, who pointed out plants that his people valued for their healing qualities, and helped her transplant some to her garden.

On Ishi's first weekend at the Giffords', she became concerned when she heard him splashing about loudly in the bathtub. Afterward, instead of the sopping wet bathroom she expected, she was pleasantly surprised to find the floor perfectly dry. The tub was spotless and the towels had been carefully folded and put away.

Letters had passed between the Bureau of Indian Affairs in Washington, D.C., and Professor Kroeber. After the Yahi had been

---

*The *kuwi* ("medicine man" in Yahi), according to Ishi, performed most of his cures by magic. He diagnosed and cured diseases by singing, dancing, blowing smoke or ashes in different directions, and pretending to suck out of the patient objects such as stones or thorns that "caused" the diseases. For ordinary ailments, medicinal roots were eaten and herbal teas drunk; usually these treatments were provided by old women.

at the museum more than a year, the bureau sent a special agent to check up on him.

The agent interviewed the professors. How was Ishi doing? Did he have any special problems? Was he learning English? Did they think he could fit into modern America?

Their replies were expressed in no uncertain terms. Ishi fitted in very well at the museum. His special knowledge was of great value to the anthropologists. Almost since his arrival he had been self-supporting. He wanted to stay and they needed him.

Next, the agent wanted to hear what Ishi himself had to say. With one of the professors interpreting, he told the Yahi that the government of the United States intended to provide for his future. It could arrange for him to return to Deer Creek and live there in peace. Or, if he preferred, he would be taken to a reservation, where he could enjoy the companionship of other Indians.

Ishi listened intently. It did not take him long to respond.

"I will live like the white man for the rest of my days," he said. "I want to stay in this place, where I am now. In this house I will grow old, and in this house I will die."

The agent shook hands and left. Time passed, a long time and a worrisome one for Ishi and his friends. Washington, it seemed, was in no hurry to make up its mind.

When it finally did, and Kroeber received the letter announcing it, he went out in search of Ishi, his face glowing with happiness.

It was spring 1914.

It was to be a vacation different from any other. In May, Kroeber, Waterman, and Pope wanted to take Ishi back to the land of his fathers, so he could show them the wilderness, the woods and creeks where he had passed his life. They told him they wanted very much to see with their own eyes how the last Yahi had lived, so they could round out their record of him and his vanished people.

Ishi frowned. Mill Creek and Deer Creek, he told them, were no place for *saldu* professors. They would have to travel far from the train, across treacherous country, and make their way down into deep canyons. Without their comfortable beds and chairs, how could they possibly manage?

Ishi's friends smiled. They were used to roughing it, they said. They would hire horses and guides to get to Yahi country. They would take along food and blankets and all the camping gear they would need.

The Indian kept shaking his head. He wanted to please his friends, but his heart was troubled. Making the trip would mean going back to the past. He had suffered hunger and privation there. He had lost those he loved best there, and many places were filled with painful memories. While here, at the museum, he had found friends and happiness again.

In the end, however, he could not talk them out of their plan, and he wasn't in the habit of saying no to them.

To live as he had in his homeland, Ishi needed certain things. In the exhibition cases of the museum were objects he had made—harpoons, bows and arrows, other things. Choosing the ones he wanted, he packed them up for the trip.

Popey had a young son, Saxton Jr.—he was eleven years old—who wanted to come along. Ishi had shown the boy how to make a bow and arrows and how to use them. The two were good friends and often practiced archery together. Popey's boy was a welcome addition to the group.

The five traveled north in a Pullman compartment. At night Ishi watched wide-eyed as the porter created places for sleeping where there had been none. Ishi asked for one of the upper berths—the notion of sleeping high up appealed to him—and he chuckled with boyish pleasure climbing up and down again and again.

Next day, the train pulled into Vina, a station close to Yahi country. As the professors said good-bye to the porter, they tipped him. Ishi gave him a quarter; having cast his lot in with the *saldu,* anything they did he would do too.

At the station, they were met by a rancher named Apperson. He supplied them with horses and pack animals; he and his son were to accompany the party as guides.

Ishi turned pale. He knew the faces of these men, and they filled him with terror. Years before, he had seen them when he lived in the wild. Six years earlier, in 1908, he had shot an arrow at Apperson, barely missing him. Wouldn't the rancher recognize him and take revenge? Men like Apperson had slain many of the Yahi, and the sight of the rancher made Ishi's blood turn to ice.

But the rancher gave no sign he had ever seen Ishi before. The Indian soon realized he had nothing to fear. A day or two later, he was chatting and laughing with the Appersons as if they were old friends. Times had certainly changed!

Ishi was confronted with another challenge. The only time he'd had anything to do with a horse was when he'd killed one and eaten it. Now suddenly he would have to ride one. He climbed up into the saddle as the others showed him, and patiently began to learn the secrets of navigating on horseback. The best course for him, he quickly realized, was to allow the horse to travel at its own pace.

Ishi had drawn a map of the area for his friends. When they came to a suitable place, they dismounted and set up camp. This was to serve them as a base; from it they planned to set out each day, returning toward evening.

In the land of the Yahi Ishi became a Yahi once more. He took off his shoes and walked barefoot. Most of the time Yahi men had gone about almost naked, so he stripped off every stitch of his clothing. All he wore was a breechclout that he made. His body, well formed and muscular, was a little softer after his years at the museum. In a few days his reddish bronze skin grew darker with the sun.

Every day Ishi and his friends went swimming in the creek. The whites swam completely in the nude. But the Indian, more modest, would not take off his breechclout.

On their first night, when everybody lay down to sleep, Ishi could not. He had to go out, he told young Saxton, whose sleeping bag lay next to his, and his voice was troubled. He had to search the canyon for the spirits of his mother, his sister, and the old man who had disappeared with her. He had not been able to perform the proper

Ishi enjoys swimming in the creek once more.

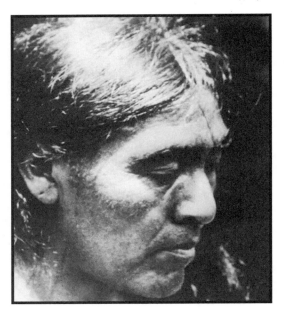

His visit to Yahi territory
sometimes brought back
painful memories.

funeral rites for them, and he was afraid their spirits might still be wandering about, unable to find the trail to the Land of the Dead.

Before dawn Ishi returned. His face was solemn, but he seemed to be more at peace.

"It is good," he told the boy. "None are lost. They found their way."

In the woods Ishi showed his companions how he hunted. He led them to a place where he said there would be deer. They watched as he held a leaf to his lips and made a sound like the bleating of a fawn. Again and again he repeated it. But no deer came.

Ishi's face grew dark. He sniffed the air. "Who smoke?" he scolded.

A deer has a keen sense of smell, he told his companions, and the odor of tobacco smoke clings to the hair and clothing a long time; no one should smoke before going out to hunt, for the smell alerts the animal to danger. His advice was heeded, and a few days later they got their first deer. Ishi skinned and butchered it with a skill born of years of experience.

On the bank of a stream, the whites watched Ishi fling his harpoon, and they had salmon for dinner. Pope often joined him in harpooning, and in hunting with bow and arrow. The others used rifles.

As they moved through the woods, every now and then Ishi would halt and squat down; before him was some plant his people had used for medicine or food. The professors made notes of these, as well as of everything else he told them or showed them.

Back at their camp, after they had dinner and washed up, they sat down around the campfire and the whites recited poems or sang. Ishi applauded with gusto. He told stories his people had related for ages and he sang their songs.

Getting to his feet, Ishi began to dance. He circled around, stamping his feet in the slow Indian way. Young Saxton got up too and copied Ishi's movements, his feet pounding the earth lustily. The

Harpoon ready, he searches the water for salmon.

others clapped their hands and swayed in rhythm. Ishi smiled. It felt like old times, almost.

Each day, as Ishi took his friends about, he told them what the places they came to had meant to him and his people. Sometimes he and his companions had to cut their way through the dense chaparral with machetes, or crawl beneath the brush. Now, for the first time, they could truly grasp the kind of life the Yahi had been forced to lead as the whites closed in all around. Ishi showed his friends where the surveyors had suddenly surprised him in 1908; where he and his fellow Yahi had escaped from the *saldu*; where he had climbed hundreds of feet, by a rope made of milkweed, up the face of a steep cliff.

Once they came to a gigantic boulder and Ishi raised his hand, signaling a stop. "Wamoloku!" he exclaimed, and he started to dig.

A few minutes later he held up some bones. They were, he told them, from a bear's paw. In that place, long ago, he had fought a bear and slain it; then he and his companions had feasted gloriously on the meat. He had buried a claw of the bear there, and the Indians had called the spot Wamoloku—"the Bear's Claw Place."

As the party moved along, they drew detailed maps, writing down the names of the places in Yahi that Ishi showed them. They compiled a photo record of Ishi and the things he did in his native setting. Painstakingly they were piling up a treasure of Yahi lore that future generations of anthropologists would thank them for.

As for Ishi, gone were the misgivings he had felt before the journey. Much of the time he was in high spirits, laughing and joking with his companions. He behaved toward them like a genial host, showing off his home to appreciative visitors.

As the vacation drew to its close, Ishi's attitude changed. He became

**Showing his old home to his
friends gave him pleasure.**

restless. True, he had been enjoying himself, but the familiar places
had called back bitter memories with the sweet. He was clearly eager to
get back to the museum and the new life he had found there.

Back at Vina, a small crowd turned out to say good-bye to the
famous Indian visitor. People held out their hands to Ishi, and he
smiled and gave each a friendly shake. While he and his companions
waited for the train, he entertained the people: he sang Yahi songs
and gave a demonstration with his bow and arrows.

This was a very different Ishi from the one who had gone off into the unknown from Oroville three years earlier. Now he could hardly wait to begin the journey, and he was the first to climb aboard the train. From the window he waved cheerily to the crowd.

"Good-boy, ladies an' genelmen!" he cried. "Good-boy!"

On the homeward trip time passed swiftly. The five friends were busy making plans: they would come back in the fall, so Ishi could show them the things the Yahi used to do in that season, when the acorns dropped to the earth. They would gather them with Ishi and see with their own eyes how a Yahi prepared for winter.

But Ishi would never come back to Yahi-land again.

In 1915 a world's fair was held in San Francisco. It was called the Pacific International Exposition, and it celebrated the winning of the West and the opening of the Panama Canal. Ishi was a featured attraction.

At the center of the fairgrounds, they placed a statue. It was called *The End of the Trail,* and it depicted an Indian on horseback. The horse looked exhausted and ready to drop. The rider, head bowed, was a forlorn and tragic figure.

Without words, it told what the winning of the West had meant to Native Americans.

During his first years at the university, Ishi's health, except for a case of pneumonia, had been excellent. During the winter of 1914—15, however, he began to fail. He showed less and less interest in shooting with his bow or even in going outdoors. He coughed, and his coughing grew worse.

In January he was admitted to the hospital. He was well known there, but not as a patient. A frequent visitor in the surgical wards, he had helped the nurses clean instruments, or entertained them and the interns with Indian songs or stories in pidgin English.

He had often joined Dr. Pope when he made his hospital rounds. Ishi also visited the sick in the wards by himself, "with a gentle and sympathetic look," said Pope, "which spoke more clearly than words." In the women's wards, with folded hands, he went from bed to bed like a doctor, "looking at each patient with quiet concern and a fleeting smile that was very kindly received and understood." Sometimes, on his visits, he sang healing songs.

This time, however, Ishi's visit was very different: he was an extremely sick man. Pope had him tested for tuberculosis. The diagnosis was negative—he appeared to have nothing more than a respiratory infection. He was treated under Pope's watchful eye. When the infection subsided, Pope discharged him. And yet . . .

In the spring Ishi was back in the hospital, this time with a hacking cough. When his lungs sounded better, he was discharged.

The respite was brief. In the summer Ishi's symptoms returned: he kept coughing, and his appetite was miserable. Back in the hospital, his lungs were examined. Now the left lung was found to be affected. He appeared to have all the symptoms of tuberculosis—and yet no tuberculosis bacilli could be detected.

The hospital seemed to be the wrong place for a person like Ishi; he pined away there. He might do better in his museum home, Pope decided. So a large, airy room was emptied of its exhibits and made ready for him.

No matter how carefully Ishi was nursed, he just wouldn't improve. He was feverish; he ate next to nothing, and grew thinner day by day. True to his Indian heritage, he never complained, but remained the same patient, good-hearted fellow he had always been.

By March 1916 Ishi was nothing but skin and bones, and so weak he had to be moved back to the hospital. He was unable to eat. He coughed all the time. Although Ishi said nothing about it, Pope could see he was in constant pain. Medication helped little.

A new hospital was being built for the university, and Ishi could see it going up from his window. He watched for hours at a time. On the steel girders the construction workers, climbing up and down, would sometimes strike clownish poses. Ishi, lying motionless, would smile at their antics.

"All a-same monkey-tee," he said.

On March 25, blood began to pour from Ishi's mouth. The hemorrhage was massive.

Pope was called. After one look at Ishi's drained, exhausted face, he pumped a large dose of morphine into him. It was the only thing he could do to help his friend—except stay by his side and watch.

He watched, helpless, as Ishi slipped away.

The Indian experts at the museum knew that when a Yahi died the remains were cremated. They had no doubt that was what Ishi would have wished for himself. In the coffin they placed the things he would expect to take with him on his last journey: five arrows with sharp points, a bow, a basket of acorn meal, some dried venison, a box of shell-bead money, a pouch full of tobacco, his fire sticks, and a few other things.

They went with Ishi to Mount Olivet Memorial Park, a cemetery near San Francisco, where he was cremated. They brought with them a small black Pueblo jar, and in this his ashes were placed. On the outside they had inscribed these words: "Ishi, the last Yahi Indian, died March 25, 1916." They set the jar inside a niche in a vault at the cemetery.

Kroeber said little about the dead Yahi. But when he did, he spoke with deep feeling. Waterman said, "I have lost the best friend I ever had."

Pope tried to console himself. "I think the closing years were far the best of his life." The image of his lost friend rose before him. "He was kind; he had courage and self-restraint, and though all had been taken from him, there was no bitterness in his heart. His soul was that of a child, his mind that of a philosopher."

A few days after the funeral, a newspaper in Chico (not far from Oroville) published some thoughts on the last "wild" Indian in North America. Briefly and pointedly it summed up the story of his life and death.

"Ishi, the man primeval, is dead. He could not stand the rigors of civilization, and tuberculosis, that arch-enemy of those who live in the simplicity of nature and then abandon that life, claimed him. Ishi . . . could make a fire with sticks, fashion arrowheads out of flint, and was familiar with other arts long lost to civilization . . . doubtless much of ancient Indian lore was learned from him. . . . He was . . . a starved-out Indian from the wilds of Deer Creek who, by hiding in its fastnesses, was able to long escape the white man's pursuit. And the white man with his food and clothing and shelter finally killed the Indian just as effectually as he would have killed him with a rifle."*

---

*In 1966, near the ruins of the old slaughterhouse outside Oroville, a monument to Ishi and his people was set up by the state. It was dedicated by an eleven-year-old boy, Jeff McInturf, who had started the movement to erect it, and Ad Kessler, a seventy-four-year-old man. Kessler was one of the butchers who found Ishi there in 1911.

Chained for Life

Brighton, on the southeast coast of England, is a jewel of a city, long famous as a seaside resort. There, on February 8, 1908, in a back room of a public house or bar, an unhappy young woman was giving birth. We know little about her beyond her name, Kate Skinner—and that she worked as a barmaid, had no money, and had no husband.

When the babies were shown to her—there were two of them and they were girls—she stared at them dumbfounded.

Although perfect in every other way, the babies were Siamese twins.

The barmaid had been much too poor to have a physician for the delivery. Instead, as often happened in such cases, an older, experienced woman helped. Her name was Mary Hilton, and she was the barmaid's employer.

For someone in Kate's position, giving birth out of wedlock—and to two abnormal children—was a double disaster. How in the world would she be able to provide for them? She was sick at heart with grief and worry.

Two weeks later, as if by magic, a good fairy appeared. This apparition was gowned neither in silver nor gold, but in the unfairylike garments of the keeper of a public house. It was Mary Hilton—and she offered to take the babies off the new mother's hands forever.

Overjoyed, Kate Skinner accepted the offer at once.

Chained for Life

Did Mary Hilton adopt the twins? She never said so. Years later, she would tell the girls she owned them—she had paid Kate for her daughters, and Kate had signed away any claim to them.

A tall, commanding woman, shrewd and grasping, Mary Hilton hadn't relieved poor Kate of her burden out of pity or the goodness of her heart. Almost from the moment she had delivered the wailing infants and discovered they were amazingly bound to each other, she had seen in them the opportunity of a lifetime.

If she played her cards right, she could transform Kate Skinner's deformed little ducklings into geese that would lay great golden eggs for her as long as she lived.

"Siamese twins" is the popular name for them. Doctors prefer to call them "conjoined twins." They are identical, which means they have the same genes and the same sex, and look just like one another.

Like other identical twins, Siamese twins develop from a single egg (or ovum), which has been fertilized by a single sperm. The egg divides, and keeps dividing, growing into an embryo.

In the case of normal identical twins, this embryo splits completely in two;* the result is two separate babies. In conjoined twins, however, the embryo stops dividing at some point—and at that point the twins remain connected.

Most Siamese twins are joined at one of three places: the buttocks, the chest, or the back. The rest are connected at some other part of the anatomy, including the head. Sometimes the twins aren't complete—one may be just part of a twin.

Around the world, about seventy thousand conjoined twins are

---

*In contrast, fraternal twins (twins who are not identical) develop from two separate eggs, fertilized by two separate sperms.

Eng and Chang, at eighteen, in 1829. They were connected by a fleshy band five inches long. Born in Siam, they were the original Siamese twins.

born each year. Then how come we don't hear about more of them? Most are dead at birth or die soon after. But not all.

One pair of conjoined twins that survived, and survived very well, were the *original* Siamese twins. Their names were Chang and Eng, and we call them Siamese twins because they were born in Siam (Thailand today). A thick thong of flesh containing blood vessels and cartilage bound them breastbone to breastbone. Because Chang and Eng became world famous, all conjoined twins born after them—as well as before—are known as Siamese twins.

Violet and Daisy, as Kate Skinner's daughters were baptized, were joined buttock to buttock, spine to spine, flesh to flesh, and blood to blood. Twins joined this way are called "pygopagus."

It's hard to imagine what it must feel like to be a Siamese twin. Perhaps normal identical twins can, for they have so much in common. But they are still two separate people.

So are Siamese twins. Almost.

Siamese twins joined like Violet and Daisy share the same life and the same destiny. They must do everything together. They must get out of bed in the morning at the same time, wash and dress together, eat, or at least sit down to eat, at the same time, go everywhere together. They must take care of their bodily functions together and go to bed at the same time—whether or not both are sleepy.

If one twin gets sick and has to be taken to the hospital, the other must go along, even though completely well. (When Daisy needed to have her appendix removed, Violet would have to lie beside her while the surgeon operated.) But we are getting ahead of our story.

The babies arrived at the crawling stage. Naturally neither could crawl about on her belly, like a normal infant; she would have had to carry her sister on her back—much too heavy a burden. The children managed anyhow: they crawled on their sides. Very quickly, as though by instinct, they began to coordinate the actions of their little arms and legs. They seemed to move about with a minimum of effort, since each girl propelled not only herself but her sister as well.

Taking their first steps was bound to give trouble. If little Violet lost her footing, Daisy had to come tumbling down with her. But learning to walk didn't take much longer for the twins than for the average toddler. They discovered they could balance each other. Four legs gave them greater stability than two could have, and they quickly learned to coordinate their leg movements. But they would never be capable of the extraordinary bursts of speed that normal children are.

In many other activities, Violet and Daisy ran into problems. Like playing, for example. When the girls were very young they loved to build houses with blocks. Each child would start to erect a house of her own, then become so absorbed in what she was doing that she would forget her sister was sitting right next to her, doing the same thing. Time and again one would make a movement that accidentally knocked down her sister's house.

It took the children a while, but they worked it out. The solution:

to take turns. One girl would build her house while the other waited. They solved many other difficulties with this approach.

Don't think the sisters didn't have plenty of tantrums along the way. If, for example, Daisy wanted to go somewhere or do something and Violet didn't, the clash of wills could be stormy. Blows would follow, and bitter tears. Until Daisy and Violet learned that if they were to do anything, one would have to give in. Sooner or later, any two people who live together must learn the same lesson. In the case of Siamese twins, sooner.

We all have moments when we need to be by ourselves—completely apart from the rest of the world. For Siamese twins, however, solitude was a luxury they could not afford. As long as both lived, neither would ever be alone.* Each had to learn to put up with the other's moods. Each had to be sensitive to the other's feelings.

Identical twins develop a deep sympathy and understanding for each other. That's because each knows the other better than anyone else in the world. This is doubly true of Siamese twins. Often they seem able to read each other's thoughts. It's not uncommon for one to finish the other's sentences.

The tight togetherness of Siamese twins gives them a unique advantage. Never, so long as they live, will either be lonesome. Someone will always be there to share one's secrets, or to lift one's spirits when they need lifting. Neither Violet nor Daisy would ever want for companionship. As children, neither would ever have to go looking for a playmate.

Sometimes children are a worry to their parents because they are slow in learning to talk. For Violet and Daisy that was never a problem.

---

*As long, that is, as they were not separated by means of surgery. But then, of course, they would no longer be Siamese twins.

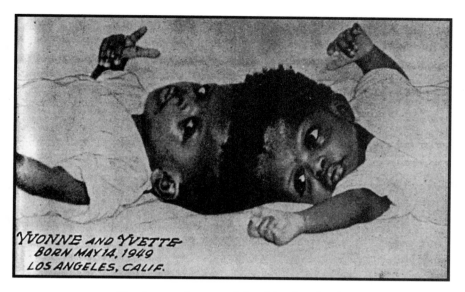

YVONNE AND YVETTE
BORN MAY 14, 1949
LOS ANGELES, CALIF.

The Jones twins were joined head to head.
Still, they managed to get about well enough.

With a sister always there to listen and comment, the twins were speaking earlier—and better—than others their age.

The girls were still in diapers when Mary Hilton set out to make her fortune with them. With her husband and her daughter, Edith, she traveled from city to city, exhibiting the twins at fairs, carnivals, and circuses—wherever there would be big crowds in a spending mood. She showed little concern for modesty, presenting their little bodies exposed so the public could see how they were connected, and also that they weren't "gaffs" (the carnival term for fakes), as some might suppose. The girls were known as "the Brighton Twins," and hordes of curiosity seekers flocked to view them.

Although little more than goslings, they were already laying golden eggs for Mary Hilton.

As small children, Violet (left) and Daisy were first exhibited in England.

■ ■ ■

One of the first words the girls learned to say was "Auntie." That was the name Mary Hilton made them call her. Her husband, by contrast, wasn't called "Uncle"; he was to be addressed only as "Sir."

Auntie took good care of her little protégés, bathing, dressing, and feeding them. So far as they could remember in afteryears, however, she never petted or kissed them. In fact, they would say she never smiled at them. Maybe she did—but most of their memories of her were bitter ones.

When Violet and Daisy were very young, they wanted to call Auntie "Mother." She soon set them straight. There was a speech she recited to them daily, over and over again— "like a phonograph," they would say.

"Your mother gave you to me. I'm *not* your mother. Your mother was afraid when you were born and gave you to me when you were two weeks old. You must always do just as I say."

When the girls were four, Auntie took them to Europe. They were exhibited in pretty dresses that were sewn together at the back; just above the connection, they wore sashes around their waists, and ribbons held their well-tended hair. They were lovely little girls, bright and cheerful, and the hearts of their audiences went out to them.

For Violet and Daisy, life was a kaleidoscope: rushed train journeys in cramped compartments, overnight stays in crowded hotel rooms, tense, hectic appearances in one foreign town after another—while Auntie, her eagle eyes sharp and critical, watched every move they made.

Auntie demanded complete obedience. If their behavior ever fell short of that, punishment followed swiftly.

"Above her waist," the girls would recall, "was always a wide leather belt, fastened with a large metal buckle, and it took only a little jerk to release the buckle. Her temper was something that her daughter or husbands [she would have five] couldn't control—and whenever we displeased her she whipped our backs and shoulders with the buckle end of that same wide belt."

From one of Auntie's husbands, the third, Violet and Daisy learned why she aimed only at these parts of their anatomy.

"She'll never hit your faces," he confided one day. "The public will not be so glad to pay to look at little Siamese twins with scarred faces."

The twins were trained, scolded, and subjected to beatings regularly. Auntie would never allow them out to play with other children. That didn't bother them. "When we looked over the sill of our room and saw little girls walking alone we felt quite sorry for them because they were not as we were."

To sit comfortably, the sisters needed a very wide chair.

■ ■ ■

Siamese twins have always held a remarkable fascination for the medical profession. Doctors were always asking to examine the girls or photograph them, and cheerfully paid for the privilege. The girls didn't care for the examinations, particularly when the doctors pinched and probed them, trying to learn more about their connection. "Double monsters," these men called them; to some, they were medical specimens rather than children with normal feelings, and when the handling got too rough they screamed and kicked. Next thing, Auntie would be calling them ungrateful brats and unbuckling her belt.

Sometimes what the doctors said upset the girls more than what they did. The surgeons in particular. Never, these gentlemen declared, had a pair of Siamese twins been separated and survived the operation.* "It would be a genuine contribution to science" if they could sever the bone, muscle, and cartilage that joined the girls, and separate the nerves of the spinal column successfully.

The girls heard, and their blood ran cold. After, they would lie sleepless in their beds, sobbing, each clasping the other's hand.

"I'll never leave you," whispered Daisy on one such night, "even though they say they can cut us apart."

"I never want to be away from you," answered her sister. To her, death seemed better than separation from her twin. "We can hold our breaths until we die."

They needn't have worried. Auntie was much more interested in golden eggs than in making a "genuine contribution to science."

Bigger and better golden eggs were what Auntie wanted. That, she knew, would take much work. And work she did; she was determined

---

*With today's improved surgical techniques and antibiotics, it has become possible to separate many—but by no means all—with good results.

to make the sisters the smartest, the most accomplished, and the most successful Siamese twins in the world.

Earlier than most children, Violet and Daisy were taught to read and write. Never permitted to associate with other children, they unconsciously copied the speech of the grown-ups around them, developing a wider vocabulary than others their age. Auntie made them memorize and recite poetry. They were given singing lessons. Daisy was taught to play the violin and Violet to accompany her on the piano. They had to practice till their fingers ached and their heads drooped.

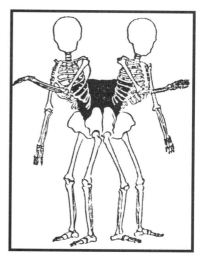

A diagram of the Hiltons' skeletons. The black area shows where they were joined by flesh and bone.

One day Auntie came upon a strange scene: Violet and Daisy standing on a chair, rocking it back and forth, harder and harder, until it turned over. As it fell, they flipped in the air and landed on their feet. Struck by their grace, she engaged a teacher to give them dancing lessons.

Little girls become big girls in time. As teenagers, the twins felt all the urges, all the need for independence that adolescents feel. Auntie, however, believed the public found younger girls more appealing; she wanted the sisters to remain children as long as possible. The twins had to put up with long curls, bows in their hair, and childish dresses (always identical) long after others their age had graduated from them.

Violet and Daisy were growing into attractive young women. Other performers and stagehands felt drawn to them and wanted to befriend them. The sisters weren't indifferent to them either. Auntie, however, refused to allow the girls to go out with them. She wouldn't even allow them to walk in the street by themselves. Why should people pay to see them, she grumbled, if they could be seen in public for nothing?

Auntie's daughter, Edith, who was older than the twins, still traveled with the show. In Australia the sisters were appearing with a circus. Before long they found their crowded hotel room was even more crowded. A young man named Meyer Rothbaum, owner of a candy and balloon concession in the circus, had become a regular caller. He was Edith's "steady," and he begged Auntie to let him marry her.

From the first, Violet and Daisy didn't take to him. His eyes, they thought, were cruel.

Auntie's husband—he was her fifth—had died. She was close to sixty now, ailing, and in need of a man to help with the show. Rothbaum could have her consent, she informed him, but only if he would give up his business and travel with her troupe. She also offered him a share in the show. So now the twins had another mentor they were expected to address as "Sir."

In his new role as a show-business impresario, Meyer Rothbaum decided he needed a show-business name. The one he chose must have seemed very stylish to him. As Meyer Meyers he made the travel arrangements, did the booking and promotion, and supervised the girls' training, just as Auntie had.

Once, perhaps to make a point, Meyers told Violet and Daisy he'd been raised by a man who had thrashed him regularly. They weren't greatly surprised. They'd already noticed he never objected when Auntie lashed out at them with her belt buckle.

Violet and Daisy gazed down at Auntie's face, strong and still handsome, framed by her carefully combed gray hair. Her lipstick was fresh and bright and the color in her cheeks good. As if by a miracle, the lines in her face seemed to have disappeared. Seldom, in all the years they had lived with her, had she looked so calm.

Somewhere an organ played softly. Auntie didn't hear it, of course. But the girls felt she might open her eyes any minute. Eyes that would look at them with calculating shrewdness and cunning. Or glare at them with a fury that could make their blood freeze.

Still, she had been their first friend—in a manner of speaking. She had taken care of them as long as they could remember.

Violet began to cry.

Daisy looked at her sister incredulously. "Why cry? We have hated her forever."

"I'm afraid without her," Violet said softly. The look on Daisy's face told her that she too was frightened.

Auntie's hands, now so peacefully folded on her breast, had held the girls in a clamp of steel. She'd exploited them, bullied them, beaten them. How many times had she said she owned them? She had treated them like slaves.

She never would again. But they knew their slavery would not end. It could even become more terrible.

The two girls had earned a fortune for Auntie. Hundreds of thousands of dollars—how many they couldn't guess. Auntie, her various husbands over the years, her daughter, and her son-in-law had lived high on the money their performances brought in. Yet the sisters barely understood what money was; Auntie had never given them any.

Between them, Daisy and Violet possessed the enormous sum of seventy-five cents. Seventy-five cents! The gift of sympathetic stage-hands, they had hoarded it for a long time. It was their nest egg.

The troupe was staying in Birmingham, Alabama. Earlier that day, Auntie's daughter had ordered the sisters to get ready quickly. They were to be taken to the funeral parlor, to say good-bye to Auntie, Edith had told them tearfully. They had hidden the nest egg in their shoes. Not much to finance a getaway. But it was all they had, and they felt desperate.

It was a moment of high hope and high anxiety. A rapid glance around revealed that Edith had collapsed in a chair and was dabbing her eyes with a handkerchief. The other slave master was busy consoling her. They appeared to have forgotten all about the twins.

"We'll never have a chance like this again," whispered Violet.

It was always difficult for them to avoid attracting attention. But now, somehow, they would have to.

They didn't look back again. They didn't dare.

"Let's run!" Daisy whispered.

And they ran, as fast as four legs would carry them.

They moved with a certain awkwardness, not very swiftly, but with a kind of speed and grace that were quite remarkable.

They hadn't taken many steps when suddenly Daisy felt a shiver run through her sister.

"Don't touch me!" cried Violet. Her voice was shrill with anguish.

Angry fingers gripped the arms of both girls.

His lips a tight line, Meyer Meyers was scowling down at them. Grasping the protesting girls firmly, he pulled them back to their seats. They slumped in them, desolate, silent.

The funeral services finally ended. Edith and Meyers brought the twins back to their room. The four sat for a long time, no one saying a word.

Violet and Daisy studied the faces that stared at them, sullen and suspicious.

The sisters, although they had many things in common, had very different personalities. Violet was the softer one. Now she burst into tears. Daisy, more independent, the leader, uttered a defiant laugh.

Edith nudged her husband. "Tell them."

Meyers took out a sheet of paper. He waved it in the sisters' faces.

"You girls belong to us now. You'll do just as we say. See here: Auntie left you to us. You and her jewelry and furniture are ours. Do you understand?"

They understood only too well. Auntie had willed them to her heirs. Like a ring, like a chair—like a thing.

From that moment, the sisters had two watchdogs to growl at them in place of one. After their attempt to escape, their new owners kept a closer watch on them than Auntie ever had. Edith and Meyers slept in the same room with the girls and never allowed them out of their sight.

The only place Daisy and Violet could be free of them was in their own minds. And, often, not even there.

The sisters now had as many reasons to complain about their new owners as they'd had about their old one. One thing they couldn't reproach Meyers with, however, was the way he promoted their act. All along they'd seen he was a better showman than Auntie—and now he made the girls' career take off.

Vaudeville in the mid-1920s already had a long history. It had begun in barrooms: a few acts, unrelated, each with one or more performers—singers, dancers, musicians, acrobats, comedians, or the like. Now it was big time, reaching across the USA, through theater chains that signed entertainers up for a series of extremely profitable engagements. Meyers launched an all-out campaign to sell the twins to the major chains, and he succeeded.

The names of Violet and Daisy Hilton soon blazed brightly in electric lights on theater marquees in one big city after another. On their first tour with the Orpheum circuit, the show included Eddie Cantor, one of Broadway's highest-paid musical comedy stars—and they would get to know other celebrities like Bing Crosby, Bob Hope (who taught them to dance the black bottom), and Harry Houdini, a famous magician. Their tours crisscrossed the country repeatedly and took the sisters around the world.

Pamphlets about the girls, sold at the theaters where they appeared, brought Meyers added money. From them we can learn some of the secrets of this clever operator.

On the cover of one pamphlet, we see a picture of the twins: Daisy seated at a piano, Violet holding a saxophone. They have warm smiles on their faces and they're fashionably dressed. On the pages inside, Meyers emphasized their beauty and their accomplishments; at the same time, he played up to the public's curiosity about their physical abnormality. He referred to them as "handicapped" and gave scientific information about their condition, explaining how they were attached. He even provided a diagram of their connected skeletons, based, he said, on "X-ray photographs."

Here's a headline from a pamphlet he sent out to publicity agents in 1926: "These Lovely Girls, Happy and Vivacious in Their Inseparably Linked Lives, Have Perfected Natural Talents Which Make Them One of the Greatest and Most Meritorious Attractions in the World." Note the word "meritorious." It was a freak show, but a freak show on a higher, educational level.

The twins' imaginative impresario had made up a fanciful story about their origins. It didn't mention the unhappy circumstances of their birth. Instead, they were described as the daughters of a British army officer, Captain Hilton. (Hilton, actually, had been Auntie's name when she bought them.) Their mother had died a year after they were born; their father had fallen in battle in Belgium, a hero, fighting the Germans in World War I. Luckily they had an "uncle and aunt," Mr. and Mrs. Meyers, who adopted the orphans. The slave owners were transformed into kindly benefactors.

Violet and Daisy, the public would read, were ideal young women who did everything that well-bred girls did. They loved to play tennis, golf, and handball; they loved to play the piano and sing; they loved to sew and to work in the kitchen; they loved to raise pets, read good books, and chat with cultured people.

Edith was referred to as their "Aunt Lou." "We have tried to show the girls every care and devotion," said Auntie the second, "and have been paid back with every ounce of love their little bodies hold."

According to her, they were very happy. She "quoted" them: "We have all the good things in life that other girls enjoy, so what more could we ask?"

True? Far from it. It was "Auntie Lou" and Meyer Meyers who had "all the good things in life." With the money Violet and Daisy had earned for them, they had bought a luxurious mansion in San Antonio, Texas, reportedly designed by America's most celebrated architect, Frank Lloyd Wright. It had stained-glass windows, a tile roof, a greenhouse, and a swimming pool. It cost seventy-five thousand dollars, when a dollar was worth many times what it is today.

"The furnishings and grounds were ornate," Violet and Daisy would say later. "And while the five acres of surrounding gardens were landscaped and strewn with lights so that a night lawn party could be given—we were never permitted to entertain any of our friends there. We could never enjoy the magnificent and splendid estate, let alone call it our own home."

Entertain their friends there? Violet and Daisy would have dearly loved to. Healthy girls with normal, healthy instincts, they were attracted to some of the young performers they met in the theater.

But, aside from brief stolen moments backstage, they could seldom even speak to them. They had never had a date, never held hands, never been kissed.

A photograph taken in 1926, when the twins were eighteen, seems to show something different. In it we see them in smart party dresses, smiling happily, as they dance with two handsome young men in evening wear. The men look as much alike as the sisters do; possibly they too are identical twins. Twins with twins—it looks like the beginning of a perfect romance.

Have we caught the watchdogs napping?

Not by a long shot. The picture was carefully posed and shot by a professional photographer working for Meyer Meyers. He used it for publicity, to project the ideal image of the sisters he wanted the public to have.

Violet and Daisy, when they saw the photo—knowing how different it was from real life—couldn't have smiled as happily as they appeared to before the camera.

As for the luxurious San Antonio mansion that Frank Lloyd Wright built—the only times the girls could live in it were when they were between tours. On those occasions Meyers promptly laid off the servants and ordered the twins to do the cleaning.

"You need exercise!" he barked at them.

Violet and Daisy, in their early twenties, were earning thousands of dollars a week. From time to time, Meyers would place a new contract in front of them and, without letting them read it, tell them to sign on the dotted lines. They had to obey.

Years earlier he'd had himself named their legal guardian, he had said. If they ever refused to do what he told them to—or tried to run away again—he had threatened to put them in an institution.

They never doubted he meant it.

Over the years the twins had wangled a few concessions out of him. Finally they had a room all to themselves. Finally they had jeweled bracelets, like other young women they knew in show business. But they were given very little money, and no freedom at all. They were never allowed to be alone with young men. When Don Galvin, a good-looking guitarist and singer, on the same bill with the twins, took Daisy's hand backstage, the clasp lasted just a second; Edith elbowed him away. When he left a bouquet of yellow roses for Daisy in the twins' dressing room, Meyers kicked it away and wouldn't let her pick it up.

Like other big-time managers, Meyers no longer handled the details of the girls' theatrical engagements. A major booking agency saw to that. The agency's advance man, William Oliver, always traveled three weeks ahead of them. It was his job to plant publicity stories in the newspapers in cities where they were scheduled to appear, and to get posters put up on billboards announcing their performance. The girls considered him a friend.

On one occasion Oliver asked them to give him an autographed picture; he wanted to send it to his wife, he said.

"To our pal Bill, with love and best wishes from your pals," one of them wrote, and both signed it.

One day in 1931 Violet and Daisy were sitting in the greenroom—a theater lounge for performers—when Meyer Meyers came hurtling in. His face was beet red.

He flung a newspaper down on a table in front of them. "Just look at this!" he bellowed.

The twins quickly learned that Bill Oliver was being sued for divorce—and his wife was charging that the twins had stolen his affections from her. She was suing them for a quarter of a million dollars.

"Why did you write 'love' on that picture you autographed for him?" Meyers said accusingly.

The twins were too dazed to answer. Meyers loaded them into his car and drove them to a lawyer's office.

Meyers informed the attorney, whose name was Andrews, that Oliver reportedly had said the twins were both in love with him. They were so jealous of each other, it was claimed, that they hadn't spoken to each other for weeks.

Meyers talked on and on, hardly giving the girls a chance to say a word.

Finally Andrews became impatient. He told Meyers to step outside; he wanted to hear the sisters' version of the story.

"You can't send me out! I'm their guardian!"

"They're over twenty-one, aren't they?" (They were twenty-three at the time.) "They don't need a guardian. Now, will you leave us?"

The door slammed behind Meyers, and the sisters were alone with Andrews. They swore there wasn't a word of truth in Mrs. Oliver's claim.

The lawyer, a kindly man, was struck by the twins' anxious, frightened looks. "Isn't something wrong?"

It was a question Violet and Daisy had been dying to hear all their lives. From the lips of both poured forth the story of how they had been held in slavery since they were babies.

Andrews was shocked. "I'll help you," he promised. "From now on, you're my clients." Dizzy with hope and excitement, the girls could hardly find words to thank him enough.

"You don't have to go home with this man," he said. The Oliver divorce suit, he assured them, was a fraud; it would not hold up in court.

To Meyers the attorney didn't say a word about his understanding with the twins.

Next, Meyers took the sisters to the home of their music teacher for a lesson. The moment he drove off, a taxi pulled up to the curb. Inside was Andrews's secretary, who had promised to meet them there.

The secretary bundled Violet and Daisy into the taxi, and they were taken to the St. Anthony Hotel, where a suite had been reserved for them. They could order anything they wanted, she said; they were Andrews's guests. She also urged them to get in touch with anybody they wanted to.

For the first time in their lives the girls were free to buy the kinds of dresses they wanted—and no two they bought were alike. They had their hair done the way they wanted. They telephoned men.

Before long they heard a knock on the door. It was Don Galvin, the guitar player.

Don kissed Daisy. Her first kiss from a young man—a man she loved! It was only on her forehead (this was a very proper young man), but both sisters were thrilled.

A few days later the twins' lawsuit to win their freedom opened in the Nineteenth District Court in San Antonio. The trial played to a packed courtroom. It was a press sensation. "Siamese Twins Unfold Tale of Bondage," proclaimed a typical headline.

The sisters won their suit hands down. Meyers's guardianship and his contract with the twins were canceled. The court awarded them one hundred thousand dollars.

At last Violet and Daisy could take charge of their own lives.

The twins' vaudeville act, now under their own management, was called the Hilton Sisters Revue. In it, they played the violin, piano, ukulele, and saxophone. They sang. They danced ballet or with male members of the troupe. They acted in sketches. And, since they were working entirely for themselves, they worked harder and performed better than ever.

Harry Houdini, master magician. He showed the sisters how to develop mental independence of each other.

■ ■ ■

The sisters had longed for romance. Now they could enjoy it to their hearts' content. They dated. They were courted. One became engaged—Daisy, to Don Galvin.

The press found the news sensational. Reporters wondered: How does Violet react while Daisy is being wooed? What thoughts run through *her* mind? What does *she* do? In an interview, newsmen put these questions to Violet. Her reply surprised them.

"Actually, I wouldn't have the least idea what was going on. Sometimes I read and sometimes I would take a nap."

When reporters asked Daisy how she felt when Violet was exchanging endearments with a boyfriend, her answer was the same. Both girls talked about the advice they had been given by Harry Houdini, the world-famous magician and escape artist, who had befriended them when they were appearing in the same theaters.

One day Houdini had found the sisters looking depressed. "Girls," he said, "character and concentration can accomplish anything for you. You must learn to forget your physical link. Put that out of your minds. Work at developing mental independence of each other. Through concentration you can get anything you want!"

Violet and Daisy had taken Houdini's advice to heart. By constant practice each had learned to concentrate so hard on what she was doing and on blocking her sister out of her thoughts, that her twin would disappear—cease to exist for her, for the time being. Thus neither would feel self-conscious because the other was present in moments that were deeply personal.

The twins' "bondage trial" in 1931 had brought them enormous publicity. That year the movie director Tod Browning—he had made the original Bela Lugosi version of *Dracula*—began work on a movie called *Freaks.* It tells the story of a group of human oddities in a circus who are mocked by other performers. The midget hero is almost poisoned by a woman acrobat who has married him for his money, but in the end he and his friends take a horrendous revenge on her and her lover. For this film Browning assembled a cast that included the most famous human curiosities of the day. Violet and Daisy were a natural choice, and a part was written into the script for them, based on their reported romances.

In Hollywood, the sisters were treated like celebrities by the movie studio; they were the center of attraction wherever they went on the set. They lived in an apartment with their maid, and they brought her to the studio every day in a big black sedan. Unlike most others in the cast, they were given a dressing room all to themselves.

"We're happier now than we have been for a long time because we're entirely on our own," they told a movie magazine. "We can do as we please, go where we please and think what we please. . . . It is so good to be free."*

---

*The motion picture *Freaks* was released in 1932. Critics and the public found it grotesque and terrifying, and it was quickly withdrawn. Thirty years later it was revived and met with a much more favorable reaction. It is still shown today.

An advertisement for the movie *Freaks*. Violet and Daisy are at top left.
In the next picture is Harry Doll, being courted by a woman who
plans to kill him for his money.

In real life the twins' romances did not fare as well as they did on
the screen.

Daisy's engagement to Don Galvin ran into problems. He was a
Mexican, and he had old-fashioned notions about a woman's role in
marriage. He wanted his fiancée to give up show business and live with
him and his family in Mexico. That, Daisy felt, would be terribly
unfair to Violet. Finally the engagement was broken off.

Violet reportedly fell in love with the twins' orchestra leader,
Maurice Lambert, and the two got engaged. When they applied for a

marriage license, it was refused. They tried again and again, with the same results. In the end, marriage bureaus in twenty-one states turned them down.

The last time was in New York City, in 1934. The comment of the city's legal counsel was typical. "The very idea of such a marriage is quite immoral and indecent. I feel that a publicity stunt was involved."*

The Blazek sisters, with Rosa's son. According to some reports she was married to the boy's father, who was killed in World War I.

After New York's refusal was reported in the press, two cities—Marion, Ohio, and Charles City, Iowa—telegraphed the rejected trio that they would be glad to provide both a marriage license and a parson. The offers were never taken up.

Stories of a new romance or an impending marriage could always get the twins into the news and help promote their act. Again and again one or the other of the sisters was reported to be on the verge of saying, "I do."

At one point, according to a newspaper article, Daisy was engaged to another orchestra leader. The twins, the article revealed, had

---

*In applying for the license, Violet pointed out that the original Siamese twins, Chang and Eng, had been allowed to marry two sisters in North Carolina. She added that another Siamese twin, Rosa Blazek, who was bound back to back to her sister Josepha, was reported to have married and become a mother. Daisy joined in her sister's plea, saying she too was engaged.

(Above) The Tocci brothers—
known as "the Two-Headed Boy"—
were two boys only down to the
sixth rib; below, they were one.
The brothers both later married.

worked out an ingenious method to take turns talking to their boyfriends—and neither sister could hear what the other was saying.

In their Texas home the twins had a one-of-a-kind telephone booth. It was constructed in such a way that one of them could shut herself inside while the other remained outside. If Violet, for example, stepped inside the booth, a panel—it was one side of the booth—was slipped down between them to the point where their bodies came together. Daisy, outside, couldn't hear, and could pass the time reading until her turn came.

Another publicity stunt?

■ ■ ■

Eng and Chang
with their wives
and two of their
twenty-one
children.

One day in 1936, the twins' publicity agent rushed in with an idea for the greatest publicity stunt of all: an actual wedding.

The twins were all for it. Violet volunteered to be the bride. Her dancing partner, James Wilson, had no objection to playing the groom. Surprisingly, the state of Texas consented.

The wedding was planned to be one of the highlights of the Texas Centennial Exposition. It was to take place in Dallas, in the Cotton Bowl, right on the fifty-yard line. Violet had a built-in maid of honor—Daisy, of course. When the best man failed to show up, the marriage party became desperate.

When the sisters married, neither had to look very far for a maid of honor.

For a substitute, they drafted the Cotton Bowl janitor. One hundred thousand guests looked on as the solemn-faced couple took their vows.

"A crowd pursued us to the door of our wedding suite," the sisters said. What happened after the door was shut on the happy trio nobody would have believed.

Inside, members of the Hilton Sisters Revue were waiting, to help them celebrate the success of the stunt they had just carried off. Present also was a special guest—the bridegroom's real sweetheart.

The wedding made newspaper front pages across the United States.

Later a brief announcement that the marriage had been annulled appeared in the inside pages.

In 1941 came Daisy's turn. She was reported to be in love with the revue's master of ceremonies, Harold Estep. He was eight years her junior. The marriage took place in Elmira, New York.

Ten days later the sisters awoke to see that the twin bed where Harold had gone to sleep the night before was empty. He never returned. Some time after, Daisy started divorce proceedings. Why had Estep deserted her? In a newspaper she read his reason for leaving.

"I guess I am not the type of fellow that should marry a Siamese twin," Estep had said. "I am not even what you would really call gregarious." (Perhaps he too should have talked to Harry Houdini!)

"The sad thing about love," said Daisy, "is, you get over it."

The press sensation caused by Daisy's marriage and separation brought the sisters to Hollywood once more. This time they had starring roles. The film, *Chained for Life*, depicted actual events in their lives. In it we see something Auntie or Meyer Meyers would never have permitted: Daisy had become a blonde!

After the peak, the valley.

The twins grew older. Their looks began to fade, and so did their appeal to theater audiences.

Vaudeville was disappearing. Touring engagements became scarcer; the sisters didn't earn as much either. There came a time—and then it came again and again—when Violet and Daisy found themselves stranded and short of cash to pay their hotel bills. Booking agents called them less and less. Finally they didn't call at all.

They'd have to try something different. But what? People, they figured, always needed to eat. With the money they had left, in 1955 they set themselves up in business in Miami, opening a hamburger stand. They called it the Hilton Sisters Snack Bar.

For some years the Siamese twins were a novelty in Miami and business was good. But after a while they found they weren't making ends meet.

They would have to give show business another try.

It was a bad move. Engagements were almost impossible to get. The twins went on the road with a carnival sideshow. After the glamour and glitter of the theater circuits, the honky-tonk cheapness of the carnival depressed them.

Middle-aged now, Violet and Daisy found themselves back where they had been as children, when they toured the English countryside, going from one fair or carnival to another. But in those days they had few worries. Auntie was in charge, and life (when she didn't punish them) was full of hope and promise.

Not anymore.

Things got harder. Fewer and fewer people were willing to pay to watch a pair of aging Siamese twins toot on their saxophones or sing and dance.

In 1962 an agent brought the sisters to Charlotte, North Carolina, for an engagement in a drive-in theater that was going to show the movie *Freaks*. After its disastrous premiere in 1932, the film had been hidden away in a vault for thirty years. Now, rediscovered, it was winning a following among the young. The sisters had been signed up to appear on the stage with it. After the last show, their agent had promised, he would be on hand to pick them up.

The last show came and went. No agent. The twins telephoned again and again. And again. The agent never returned their calls.

Violet and Daisy had been in Charlotte in happier times. In 1945. That was when vaudeville was still alive in some places, and theater audiences still applauded. The press made a fuss over them; they were interviewed and they posed for photographs. The sisters chattered away cheerfully, reeling off pat phrases supplied by their agent.

"We may seem like one," they said, "but everything costs us for two. We pay insurance for two, but could only collect for one. The only bargain we get is our weight for a penny." (They weighed 166 pounds, the interviewer reported; they were four feet nine inches tall.) But that was then and this was now. Then the twins were still riding high.

Violet and Daisy rented a trailer. They were running low on money. A good-hearted neighbor sometimes invited them into her trailer for meals. That helped.

Surprisingly, someone still believed they had possibilities. The owner of a supermarket chain hired them, and they were put to work in a new kind of job for them—weighing produce. Except for their stage clothes, they had hardly anything to wear. The owner bought them dresses that were better suited to their new employment. Their kindly neighbor would recall that "they came and sat on my couch and fixed 'em so they could wear 'em."

Like so many other human oddities, Violet and Daisy were survivors. Most Siamese twins, we have seen, die early. But the sisters, from the day they were born, had tremendous vitality. Abused, dragged around the world, painfully conscious of how different they were from other human beings, they had developed the ability to adapt to circumstances. It was sink or swim, and they had learned how to swim.

But they had changed with the years. Earlier they had been outgoing, eager to make new friends, interested in everything. By now they had become very private individuals. They did join a local church and attend Sunday services. At the Park-N-Shop, where they worked, they were well liked by their fellow employees and by their regular customers. But they would hardly ever talk about the colorful lives they had led as entertainers and sideshow curiosities, although people would have dearly loved them to.

It was 1968, almost Christmas. The twins called in sick. Days passed, and not a word from them.

By January 4 their friends still hadn't heard from them. When they telephoned, there was no answer. They became very worried. That night they came over to check.

No one responded to the doorbell. They rang and rang. When they finally got inside, they wished they hadn't. On the floor they saw the sisters. They were huddled against each other, silent, unmoving, cold.

Long ago, when the twins were children, they had overheard surgeons saying they wanted to sever them one from the other. The girls had been terrified at the thought of the operation, of being divided from each other. They would rather have died than be separated.

"I'll never leave you," Daisy had told her sister.

"I never want to be away from you," Violet had replied.

Their most precious wish had been never to be parted. Out of so many wishes, that one, at least, had been granted.*

Four days later, under a gloomy gray sky, the sisters were laid to rest in Charlotte's Forest Lawn Cemetery. About sixty mourners looked

---

*The Hilton sisters appeared to have died of the Hong Kong flu. Their circulatory systems were connected, so if one contracted an infectious disease, the other would always get it. At the time of their death they were sixty years old. At least two other pairs of conjoined twins have lived longer: the original Siamese twins, Chang and Eng, who were sixty-two when they died, and Millie-Christine, known as "the Two-Headed Nightingale," who were sixty-one.

Millie-Christine, known as "the Two-Headed Nightingale," were connected somewhat like the Hilton sisters. Born into slavery, they earned a fortune for their master before the Civil War.

on, some red-eyed and sniffling. Many had been customers of the sisters or had known them from the church. All of the employees of Park-N-Shop turned out; six of them served as pallbearers, carrying the standard-sized coffin to the grave.

At the religious service before, the coffin had not been opened; the few curiosity seekers who came were denied a last gawk at the twins. "I wonder which one died first," said one woman.

Later the twins' minister, the Reverend Sill, revealed he had searched through the twins' possessions; they had left a $2,800 estate, and he hoped he might find a clue to a relative to inherit it. He could find none. But he did discover letters that reflected the turbulent lives the sisters had led.

Violet and Daisy, he recalled, had bought gifts for their regular customers every year. "Even this Christmas" —when they were already ill— "they sent their presents to the store to be passed out."

"I think the sisters were happiest here in Charlotte," the minister said. "They were eager to appear, for once in their lives, as something other than freaks."

The Pygmy in the Cage

Saturday, September 8, 1906.

At the Bronx Zoo (also known as the New York Zoological Park) something very peculiar was going on.

Something no one had ever seen in the zoo's history.

Something that, after a few days, no one would ever see there again.

At the zoo, attendance had been dropping off. It always does in September, as the warm days of summer become fewer and cool breezes begin to blow. But today, instead of the handful of visitors you might expect to see outside the crescent-shaped enclosure next to the monkey house, a large crowd had gathered. Men, women, and children were peering excitedly between the metal bars of the fence—and from minute to minute their numbers were growing.

One often saw crowds at the monkey house. Nothing seems to amuse human beings so much as the antics of their simian relatives. But, for this time of year, the size of the crowd was definitely unusual. The people's mood was unusual too. They kept pointing and gesturing, or laughing out loud. From time to time a many-throated cheer burst from them.

In a cage not far away, a shaggy-maned old lion gave a deep roar, as if it resented the rival attraction.

Something was up at the monkey house—no doubt about it.

The Pygmy in the Cage

That something was a human being on exhibition inside the enclosure. His skin was brown and he was remarkably short—so short he might be taken for a dwarf. All he had on was trousers and a jacket, beneath which his naked skin showed. His feet were bare.

He certainly wasn't a zookeeper. A short distance away you could see the actual keeper (his name was Engelhome). His eyes, friendly but alert, watched every move the little fellow made.

The dark-skinned man was holding a bow almost as long as he was, and from his shoulder hung a quiver of arrows. He fitted one to the bowstring. He squinted, taking aim at a target at the other end of the enclosure. It wasn't the familiar bull's-eye type but a makeshift one of heaped-up straw.

The bowstring twanged, and the arrow buried itself in the straw.

The crowd cheered.

The keeper, someone noticed, had slipped out of the enclosure and was carefully locking the door behind him.

He reappeared shortly with something in his hand. The sun glinted on a soda-pop bottle as he held it out to the dwarflike man. He took it, tipped it up to his mouth, and emptied it in almost a single swallow. The crowd roared in amusement, as if it had never seen anyone empty a soda-pop bottle before.

The little fellow must have found the crowd's behavior as amusing as it found his own. He laughed back at the spectators. Between his lips they could see a mouth full of shining white teeth.

Immediately they noticed something very odd about them: Each tooth had been filed to a point, forming a triangle.

A cannibal, somebody said. No one but a cannibal would file his teeth like that.

All at once the little man stopped shooting. An animal, hairy and

Smiling broadly, Ota exhibits his filed teeth. People thought he was a cannibal.

black, had emerged from the monkey house. It was a young chimpanzee, and it was moving on all fours toward him.

Chimps have remarkably expressive faces; this one's looked completely miserable and woebegone. When the chimp was close to the man it stopped and squatted on its haunches, its eyes were fixed on his face.

The man, who had resumed shooting, pretended not to notice.

The animal whimpered. Then the whimper grew louder. It almost sounded like a child crying.

The dark-skinned man laid down his bow. Strange sounds came from his mouth. Could they be words? If so, they were spoken in a language no one present had ever heard before. The tone of his voice was soft and sympathetic.

At once the ape swung its body on its long arms and loped across the space that separated it from the man. Reaching him, it rubbed its muzzle against his leg.

Bending over, the man scooped up the animal. It nestled against his breast and fastened its right arm across his chest, its left over his shoulder. Its long legs clamped themselves firmly to his body. The whimpering died away as he patted it affectionately.

The Pygmy in the Cage

After a bit he carried the chimpanzee toward the monkey house and disappeared through a doorway. The crowd waited for him to reappear. When he didn't, they surged toward the entrance of the building, the children scampering and yelling in front.

The large space in the center of the monkey house quickly filled with people. All around were cages, and the cages were alive with monkeys of different sizes and colors, all engaged in various kinds of monkey business. Some swung from horizontal bars, grimacing; some sat in corners grooming one another quietly, like schoolgirls; some shrieked as they chased one another up and down the bars of the cages; others nibbled at the carrots, bananas, lettuce leaves, or other food that littered the floor.

One large ape had a cage all to itself. Regular zoo visitors knew the creature well: its name was Dohong, and it was the star of the monkey house. Many zoos had not yet learned that it was better to let animals be animals, but trained some of them to perform as they do in the circus. Dohong was one of these. He could dress himself, putting on trousers, a jacket, and a cap. Today his long coat of brick red hair was hidden beneath his best suit, and he was riding back and forth on a tricycle, the most solemn expression imaginable on his long face.

But today no one had eyes for Dohong. The crowd wanted the unusual little black man with the pointed teeth. It found him in a cage at one end of the building. He was sitting on a hammock, busily weaving straw into what appeared to be a mat. His face was a mask of concentration as his fingers moved deftly back and forth.

A child called out to him. He bared his teeth in a broad grin.

The crowd was pressing up against the cage, laughing and chattering, much like the monkeys. No one had ever seen a man in a cage before, except possibly at carnivals, where fake "wild men" were sometimes exhibited.

But this little fellow was something entirely different, keeper Engelhome said. He was a Pygmy.

A Pygmy! Some had heard of these fabled little folk who dwelled in the mysterious jungles of the Dark Continent, as Africa was known. A few had even read about them in the writings of explorers like H. M. Stanley and David Livingstone. But no one there had ever expected to see one in the flesh.

This is better than a sideshow, someone said. The crowd's boisterous laughter bounced from wall to wall.

But not everyone was happy about the spectacle. "Even those who laughed the most," observed a reporter in the *New York Times* the following day, "turned away with an expression on their faces such as one sees after a play with a sad ending."

"Something about it that I don't like," he heard a man in the crowd say.

The little man, however, didn't mind at all. He continued to play happily with the apes and monkeys at the zoo, entirely unaware of the storm that was about to break around him.

P. T. Barnum, founder of "the Greatest Show on Earth."

If some in the crowd were displeased by the show, William T. Hornaday, the zoo's director, wasn't one of them.

Hornaday, a distinguished zoologist, had a little of the old-time showman P. T. Barnum about him. Barnum, sometimes called the father of the American circus, first made himself famous by exhibiting human oddities—creatures very different from the ordinary human being. Especially notable were the midget General Tom Thumb Jr. and "the Feejee mermaid," who was not a mermaid at all (there aren't any) but a curiosity created by attaching a fish's tail to a monkey's torso.*

Now, borrowing a page from Barnum's book, Hornaday was attempting to draw greater crowds to his zoo by exhibiting a Pygmy—the first one New York had ever seen.

On Saturday, the large number of visitors had been attracted by publicity that the zoo would have a one-of-a-kind feature at the monkey house. On Sunday a horde descended on the zoo. Drawn by word of mouth and the *Times* article—it was headlined "Bushman Shares a Cage with Bronx Zoo Apes"—it numbered in the thousands. Many were delighted with the unusual sight they found there.

General Tom Thumb, one of Barnum's greatest attractions, with his wife and a child.

At the front of the Pygmy's cage they beheld a sign:

THE AFRICAN PYGMY, "OTA BENGA." AGE, 23 YEARS. HEIGHT, 4 FEET 11 INCHES. WEIGHT, 103 POUNDS. BROUGHT FROM THE KASAI RIVER, CONGO FREE STATE, SOUTH CENTRAL AFRICA BY DR. SAMUEL P. VERNER. EXHIBITED EACH AFTERNOON DURING SEPTEMBER.

Although many enjoyed the man-and-monkey exhibition, others, as we've seen, objected to it. African Americans, in particular, were deeply offended to see a black man exhibited with an ape.

"The person responsible for this exhibition," the Reverend Dr. R.

---

*A fuller account of these curiosities and the career of P. T. Barnum may be found in *Very Special People: The Struggles, Loves, and Triumphs of Human Oddities* (Citadel Press, 1991), by Frederick Drimmer.

S. MacArthur of Calvary Baptist Church told the press, "degrades himself as much as he does the African. Instead of making a beast of this little fellow, he should be put in a school for the development of such powers as God gave to him."

Dr. MacArthur announced he was getting in touch with other black ministers. The display was a disgrace, and they would put an end to it.

At the zoo that Sunday, Ota had been given a pair of canvas shoes. To make the show more interesting, Dohong the orangutan had been placed in the enclosure with him. Ota, who had never seen orangutans before,* was attracted to the ape. The ape was equally attracted to him. The two frolicked together like old friends. Often they were locked in each other's arms, or they wrestled playfully. They put on a good show, and the crowd loved it.

When Ota returned to the cage inside the monkey house, he seated himself on a stool. He often looked down at his new shoes. The crowd decided the "savage" was admiring them, and that made them howl. The Pygmy busied himself weaving something with a ball of twine. Engelhome had placed himself close to the front of the cage.

What was the Pygmy making, the crowd wanted to know.

A hammock, Engelhome informed them; he's very good with his hands. He and Ota were quite "chummy," the keeper said.

The little man glanced up from his work. He smiled good-naturedly at the crowd, which couldn't take its eyes off him and his strange teeth.

Some older boys were standing up front. One of them put two fingers in his mouth and suddenly emitted a piercing whistle. Another gave a catcall, loud and mocking.

Ota's head jerked up. The pleasant smile dissolved on his face. His handsome features twisted into a grimace; he looked almost ugly. The

---

*Orangutans are found only in Borneo and Sumatra.

The Pygmy in the Cage

Pygmy jumped to his feet, and his handiwork dropped from his lap. A stream of furious words poured from his mouth, some in pidgin English, some in his African language.

What was the little man so angry about, somebody asked Engelhome.

"He says they're making fun of him." The keeper shook his head.

Across the front of the cage hung a drawn-up curtain. Its bottom was low enough for Ota to reach, and now, his eyes blazing, he reached for it. In one quick sweep of his arm, he pulled it down, hiding himself completely from view.

The show was over.

What is a Pygmy—and how had one come to be on exhibition in a cage at the Bronx Zoo?

The story is a fascinating one.

Everybody knows that Pygmies are small people—but just how small are they? An adult male doesn't grow to more than fifty-nine inches. That, we've seen, was exactly Ota's height. The average Pygmy, however, is at least a few inches shorter, and female Pygmies are shorter than males. Pygmies aren't dwarfs.*

Pygmies live in small bands in the tropical rain forests of Africa. Each band has its own territory and its own chief, usually the band's best hunter. Pygmies have reddish brown skins and curly brown hair. They are an ancient people; some anthropologists believe they are the ancestors of all mankind. Today there are about two hundred thousand of them.

The Pygmies are greatly outnumbered by the taller Africans, who speak Bantu and moved in long ago. Unlike their tall neighbors, who

---

*The shortness of dwarfs is usually caused by a genetic disorder (in the case of midgets, a hormone deficiency). The shortness of Pygmies is racial.

are farmers and herders, the Pygmies lead a more primitive life—they are food gatherers and hunters, and daring ones at that. They live mainly on the flesh of birds, deer, monkeys, and other animals (elephants among them), as well as insects, bananas, and other food that grows in the wild. They are not the slow-witted, backward creatures they were believed to be in Ota's time, but are intelligent and capable.

The Pygmies have formed close relationships with their taller Bantu-speaking neighbors. They exchange meat and wild honey with them for rice, fruits and vegetables, knives, and other products, and sell their Pygmy daughters to them as wives. The little people have also adopted their language. As the taller tribes cut down the trees to clear land for their crops and herds, the rain forest keeps shrinking, and with it the homeland of the Pygmies.

Samuel Phillips Verner, the man who brought Ota Benga from Africa, was an explorer. The grandson of a South Carolina slave owner, he had studied for the Presbyterian ministry and become a missionary. A very modern one, however: he had read the writings of Charles Darwin and was a firm believer in the theory of evolution.

In 1896, Verner, in his early twenties, made his first trip to Africa as a missionary. The Congo Free State (Zaire today) was then ruled with a hard hand by the Belgians. There he learned a local language, Tshiluba, so he could give the word of God to the natives in their own language. He also contracted malaria, a disease that for the rest of his life would lay him low with fits and fevers from time to time. When he came back to America in 1898, with him he brought monkeys, parrots, a wildcat, plants, battle-axes, and other colorful articles—and two full-sized Africans eager to visit the wonderful land he had told them about.

The Pygmy in the Cage

Verner's second trip, in 1903, was very different. This time he didn't go as a missionary; he'd been hired as a special agent of the world's fair that was to be held in St. Louis the following year. His job was to bring back some Pygmies and other natives to be exhibited at the fair.

Traveling through the jungle, Verner reached the village of a warlike tribe, the Baschilele. In the slave market there, his eyes fell on the sad little figure of a Pygmy who was being offered for sale. Verner had no sympathy with slavery. It cost him just a bolt of cloth and a pound of salt to buy the Pygmy's freedom. The little man's name was Ota Benga.

For Ota, his rescue by the good-hearted *muzungu* ("white man") was a godsend. His captors ate human flesh—and he had expected to be given the place of honor on one of their menus.

Such an end wouldn't have surprised Ota too much. Lately his life had been nothing but a string of misfortunes. Belgian troops, in search of ivory, had failed to find any in his village, and in revenge had burned it to the ground. Ota had been away on an elephant hunt; when he returned, he discovered the butchered bodies of his wife and his two children. He and the surviving members of his band were taken captive, and he had been turned over to the Baschilele.

Now, suddenly, things were looking up for him.

They weren't, exactly, for his rescuer. Verner still hadn't gotten the Africans he needed for the fair, and his time was running short. Taking Ota with him, he approached a tribe of Pygmies known as the Batwa. To any who would be willing to travel to America with him, he promised rich rewards.

No takers. After being mistreated by the Belgians, the Batwa wanted nothing to do with the white man and his white world.

Now, at Verner's side, Ota Benga spoke up. He'd had long talks about America with Fwela ("the leader," the name by which Verner was known), he told them. He himself hungered to see the wonders of the New World. Fwela, he said, had saved his life and could be trusted: Fwela would take good care of them and bring them back home to their village. They would become heroes among their people.

In the end, four young men agreed to go. With them went Ota Benga and three full-sized Africans.

The St. Louis Exposition of 1904 was the biggest fair America had ever seen. Eighteen million people attended it. Yet today hardly anyone remembers it. Except for a song:

> Meet me in St. Louis, Louis,
> Meet me at the fair,
> Don't tell me lights are shining
> Any place but there.

The exposition celebrated the hundredth anniversary of the Louisiana Purchase. It was, of course, one year late. The purchase, made by President Thomas Jefferson in 1803, doubled the territory of the new nation—it added to it all the land stretching from the Mississippi to the Rockies, from Canada to the Gulf of Mexico. At fifteen million dollars it was the biggest bargain in American history.

One of the fair's most striking features was a gigantic exhibition of unusual peoples from around the globe. Americans were to have a very special experience; they would see in one place races as different as the Ainus of Japan, Eskimos, Patagonians from the tip of South America, Igorots and Moros from the Philippines, fifty different Indian tribes (including Apaches, led by the legendary warrior Geronimo), Zulus, and a host of others. Among them would be Ota Benga and the four Batwa Pygmies.

Inside their enclosure, the Pygmies wore little more than their loincloths, lived in simple huts like those at home, and busied themselves doing the things they did at home. With their strange filed teeth, they were one of the fair's greatest novelties. (Newspapers repeatedly mentioned their teeth as proof the little people were cannibals.) Visitors couldn't stop staring at these odd creatures, who had never been seen in America before.

The little people had brought with them their pet monkeys and parrots for company. Now they watched with anguish as their animals perished because of "lighted cigars and other vicious gifts forced on them by too-attentive visitors," as a newspaper reported.

The Pygmies suffered too. Verner gave lectures about them to the crowds, but the visitors couldn't

Geronimo, the Apache chief, was called "a true wild man," during his war with the U.S. Army. Ota made his acquaintance at the fair.

keep their hands off the little people, feeling their bodies and pinching them as if they were less than human. Occasionally the police had to be called to their rescue.

The Pygmies quickly discovered money and what they could get with it. Like people in foreign lands around the world, they started to charge visitors who wanted to take their pictures.

On July 2 the *St. Louis Post-Dispatch* reported that Ota (he was described as a "cannibal") "had his photo taken today and held his

Ota Benga, second from left, stands with his fellow Pygmies at the fair while a monkey begs for attention.

hand out for recompense. He received a five-cent piece with a very poor grace and wanted more. He produced a very smart, civilized-looking purse and hid away his wage with his other wealth. He had nearly half a dollar already. Then he lit his cigarette and inhaled in huge breaths with the greatest delight, babbling volubly in the Baluba [Tshiluba] language."

Later in July a gala event took place: some of the unusual peoples on exhibition performed native dances in the fair's Plaza St. Louis. The Pygmies and their fellow Africans decided to do a war dance as a special treat for the visitors. Brandishing spears, bows, and arrows, they uttered bloodcurdling battle cries. Fierce scowls on their faces, they began to advance on the spectators. Their menacing gestures made it look as if they were really going to charge.

There was only a handful of the Africans, of course. But stories that they were savages and eaters of human flesh had been read by the public again and again.

Women screamed. The densely packed crowd of fairgoers was instantly transformed into a raging mob. They pushed forward against the line of guards standing between them and the Africans, crying out and shaking their fists.

The black men huddled together, their faces distorted in terror.

The Pygmy in the Cage

**The Africans dance for the crowd.
Ota, his back to the onlookers, is at the right.**

Luckily the line of guards held. A detail of militia arrived on the double and the crowd broke up.

For Verner, as for St. Louis, the fair was a great success. It awarded the explorer a grand prize for bringing the Africans to the fair. In 1905, keeping his promise, he took them back home.

In the Batwa village, the tribe members were intensely curious to learn what their kinsmen had been doing in America. The returned travelers put on a show to explain.

First they erected a wooden pen. Inside it they set Verner's rocking chair and his table, with his phonograph and some books and papers upon it. Then they asked Verner to step inside. Obligingly he sat down in the chair, lit his pipe, and began to smoke. He played a record. He wrote on the paper. He read a book.

The Pygmies outside the fence looked on in bewilderment. They finally got the idea when the returned travelers explained that the villagers outside were the white people, and Verner represented the Pygmies—and that's how it had been in America.

After returning the Pygmies to their village, Verner turned his mind to his main goal: making his fortune. He intended to collect elephant tusks, unusual artifacts, rare plants and insects, wild animals—anything museums and zoos back home might buy.

Ota wanted very much to join his friend Fwela in his expeditions, and Verner said he'd be glad to have him along. But the little man had never gotten over the loss of his murdered family, so first he took himself another wife among the Batwa. In between his trips with Verner, he spent time with his bride and went out hunting.

A year later Verner decided it was time to go home. He had bought many things to sell in the United States. He was running out of money and he'd been away from his wife and children too long. He broke the news to Ota.

Ota's face turned gray. It was a hard blow. And it came on top of one even harder. A poisonous snake had sunk its fangs into his little wife. He had barely found her; now, suddenly, she was gone.

And now he was about to lose his friend Fwela. Fwela, who had saved him from the eaters of men. Fwela, who had taken him across the great water and back.

To Ota, Fwela was the most wonderful person in the world. His dearest wish was to be like his white friend. Fwela was a master of magic. Fwela could heal. Fwela could read mysterious messages marked on paper. If only Ota could master reading and writing! That would, he believed, give him some of Fwela's great powers. Through Fwela he could learn the other magical secrets of the *muzungu*.

Ota often made believe he was Fwela. Like other Pygmies, he had a remarkable gift for mimicking those around him. When Verner wasn't looking, Ota imitated him. He would pretend to smoke Fwela's pipe, to read his books, to write a letter. Doing these things, he hoped, would give him some of Fwela's powers.

So close had the little man grown to his tall white friend, he felt that if Verner left he did not want to go on living.

Verner would never forget the words Ota used to tell him that.

Refuse to take me with you, Fwela, he had said in a quiet voice, and I'll throw myself in the river.

Verner could see he meant it.

It didn't take Ota long to get ready. He didn't need much more than a mat, a few sacred amulets, and his bow and arrows. To relieve the boredom of the long ocean voyage, he often amused himself with a chimpanzee and a parrot, two of the animals Verner was taking with him to sell.

The odd couple and the crates of animals and artifacts arrived in New York City in August 1906. One of Verner's first stops was at the vast brownstone home of the American Museum of Natural History, where he called on the director, Harmon C. Bumpus. Verner told him of the valuable animals and objects he had brought with him, and he offered Bumpus his pick. Verner needed money fast; with his extensive knowledge of the Congo, he said, he could be very useful to the museum in a staff position. Bumpus said he'd think it over.

Could he leave his collection at the museum while he went South to visit his family, Verner asked. Bumpus agreed. Could he also leave Ota Benga? It would be, he said, a grand opportunity for the museum's anthropologists to study a Pygmy firsthand. Bumpus agreed again, and the explorer departed.

Ota had arrived at the museum with little more to wear than a native skirt. "I have bought a duck suit for the Pygmy," the director wrote Verner. "He is around the museum, apparently perfectly happy, and more or less a favorite of the men." Ota, it seems, made friends wherever he went.

The Pygmy was fascinated by the huge museum. With its astonishingly lifelike exhibits of animals from all over the world, its meteors, priceless gems, bizarre dinosaur skeletons, native weapons, and whatnot, it was a wonderland for a bright, curious fellow like Ota. His new friends were enormously interested in him too. He posed patiently while a sculptor made a bust of the unusual visitor. A museum treasure today, it does not bear Ota's name, but just a single word: "Pygmy."

Up to now Ota's life had been very active, lived almost entirely in the out-of-doors. After the first weeks, the novelty of the museum wore off. He felt terribly out of place in its close, confined corridors and galleries, where no one could speak his language.

Where was Fwela? Was he never coming back?

One day, museum guards, inspecting a group of departing visitors, saw a small black man in a white duck suit moving toward the exit among them. He looked very familiar. In a moment they caught up with him. Sure enough, it was Ota Benga. He went back with them readily enough. Perhaps all he'd wanted was a breath of fresh air. Or perhaps he'd been on his way out to look for Fwela.

Museums need money to keep going, lots of money. Usually they depend upon wealthy patrons to support them. The vast American Museum of Natural History, with its great collections and numerous staff, was no exception. A rarity like a Pygmy fresh from the jungle, Bumpus realized, would certainly appeal to his millionaire patrons. He couldn't wait to invite them to meet Ota.

Among the important guests at the museum that day were Daniel Guggenheim, a Wall Street tycoon, and his wife. Bumpus presented Ota to them.

Here is a man, said Bumpus, "whose people have not yet progressed even to the need for stone."

"Well, I couldn't interest him in shares of aluminum, could I?" replied the financier with a smile. There was laughter all around.

Ota understood nothing of what was being said. But he could read faces, gestures, and voice tones well enough. He felt that people were making fun of him, and he didn't like it.

Mrs. Guggenheim was standing, and Bumpus figured he could score points by getting Ota to bring her a chair. Indicating one on the other side of the room, he told Ota to bring it over for her; he showed by gestures what he meant.

His filed teeth bared in a smile, Ota went up to the chair. He raised it, took careful aim, and flung it toward her. It landed with a crash close to where the woman was standing. She stood speechless, openmouthed.

All conversation in the room had died. Then suddenly the room was full of the babble of shocked voices.

Ota had disappeared.

Bumpus, who had seen Ota leave, rushed after him. He found the Pygmy in his favorite place. It was in the geology hall, and Ota was perched on top of a huge meteor.

In a loud, stern voice Bumpus ordered the Pygmy to come down. Ota wouldn't—not until he was good and ready.

An urgent letter from Bumpus was delivered to Verner. His Pygmy was restless, the director told him angrily; his animals needed attention too. How soon could he take them off the museum's hands?

Verner could see his dream of a museum career had gone up in smoke. Taking the train back to New York, he picked up Ota and the fifty cases he'd left in the director's care.

His next port of call was the Bronx Zoo. There the director, Hornaday, shook his hand warmly. Not only was he ready to buy some of Verner's animals; he was intrigued by the Pygmy. When Verner told him he needed to get back to the South, Hornaday said he'd be happy to take care of the little man.

And that was how Ota Benga came to be on exhibition in a cage at the Bronx Zoo on Saturday, September 8, 1906.

Sunday, September 9.

The first sign of trouble had come with the opening of Ota's exhibition the day before. It had begun with the forceful complaint by Dr. MacArthur of the Calvary Baptist Church, who had watched the display with disgust that "the zoo was making a beast of the little fellow."

Newsmen know when they are onto a good thing. After interviewing MacArthur, they promptly called on Dr. Gilbert of the Mount Olivet Baptist Church.

Dr. Gilbert was very upset. The exhibition, he declared, was a disgrace. He said he and other church leaders were joining with Dr. MacArthur to see to it the Pygmy was released from the cage and placed in more suitable surroundings.

Dr. Hornaday wanted to put out the rising flames. He didn't exactly know how.

"This is the most ridiculous thing I've ever heard of," he told the press. He'd placed the "boy" in a cage simply for the convenience of the thousands who wanted to see him. "Why, we are taking excellent care of the little fellow and he is a great favorite with everybody connected with the zoo. He has one of the best rooms in the primate house."

The Pygmy in the Cage

On Monday, September 10, the Colored Baptist Ministers' Conference gathered in an emergency meeting. They wanted action—and they wanted it fast. To get it, they appointed a committee to go to City Hall, call on Mayor George McClellan, and get him to put a stop to the exhibition. Dr. James H. Gordon, superintendent of the Howard Colored Orphan Asylum in Brooklyn, was named chairman. If the mayor refused to free their little brother, the ministers said, they would call a public protest meeting.

Dr. Gordon and his fellow ministers hurried to the zoo—they wanted to see Ota for themselves, and how he was being treated. The sign describing him was still up, but Ota's performance had been called off for the afternoon. The Pygmy was still in his cage, however, and with him was his new friend, Dohong.

How was the zoo treating him, the ministers asked Ota. His only answer was a smile. (Either he had no objections, or he hadn't understood.)

Why had Dr. Verner placed him in the zoo, the ministers asked Hornaday.

Verner didn't have any other place to leave him, they were told.

"Dr. Verner," retorted Superintendent Gordon, "didn't apply to the proper persons. We have two hundred twenty-five children in the institution to which I belong—some of them pretty large children. We will take this little African and be pleased to have him. . . . If this does not suit, I will take him personally into my house and be responsible for him to the fullest extent. . . .

"Our race, we think, is depressed enough without exhibiting one of us as apes. We think we are worthy of being considered human beings, with souls. . . ."

Dr. Hornaday now saw he would have to give ground. No exhibitions would be held on Sunday again, he said; he didn't want to hurt anyone's feelings. But that was as far as he would go. He intended to continue the exhibit unless the New York Zoological Society ordered him to stop. "I do not wish to offend my colored brothers' feelings. . . . It is my duty to interest the visitors to the park."

That, of course, did nothing to calm the indignant ministers, who went to call on the mayor the following day.

At City Hall, on Tuesday, the clergymen found themselves facing another stone wall. "The Mayor Won't Help to Free Caged Pygmy," the New York Times would headline its report of the visit.

The ministers had been kept waiting a long time outside the mayor's office. Finally his secretary emerged. His Honor was "too busy" to see them, he reported; also, McClellan could do nothing to help because he had "no jurisdiction" over the zoo. They should take their complaint to the New York Zoological Society, he suggested.

They did. At the society's headquarters, an executive gave them a polite but weasel-worded reply: he'd like to help, but he couldn't promise anything.

The zoo, the ministers could see, was enjoying a great surge of popularity—and as long as Ota continued to draw the crowds, the society would do nothing to halt the exhibition.

But the ministers certainly would. They ordered their lawyer to take their case to court and make things hot for the zoo.

Ota must be set free.

If the ministers weren't pleased by the mayor's reply, Director Hornaday was. He wrote Mayor McClellan a letter of thanks. The whole business, he said, was "a newspaper sensation, created out of nothing, by a very bright reporter on the Times." He charged the reporter with personally arousing the ministers.

But the tide was turning. The newspapers, at first intrigued by the new exhibit, soon began to criticize it. The *New York Times,* in an editorial, declared that "we do not know of any measurable benefits to science that will accrue from the continued display of Ota Benga as the playmate of an orangutan. Not a few people are coming to look sourly on menageries, anyhow, and to wonder if they are worth while. Those who believe in them, therefore, should be particularly careful to respect the public's sensibilities, and to heed its opinions and even its prejudices."

The *New York Journal* hit out at the zoo authorities strong and hard:

THE BLACK PIGMY IN THE MONKEY CAGE AN EXHIBITION IN BAD TASTE, OFFENSIVE TO HONEST MEN, AND UNWORTHY OF NEW YORK CITY'S GOVERNMENT.

The gentlemen in charge of the Zoological Garden in the Bronx have again illustrated the foolishness of allowing semi-official busybodies to manage public affairs.

These men—with good intentions probably, but without thought and intelligence, have been exhibiting in a cage of monkeys, a small human dwarf from Africa.

Their idea, probably, was to inculcate some profound lesson in evolution.

As a matter of fact, the only result achieved has been to hold up to scorn the African race, which deserves at least sympathy and kindness from the whites of this country, after all the brutality it has suffered here. . . .

It is an absolutely shameful disgrace to every man in any way connected with it, and this newspaper indorses most earnestly the action of clergymen and others of the Afro-American race in protesting so vigorously against it.

After just a few days, Ota was withdrawn from exhibition. His home was still the monkey house, but people could no longer watch him behind bars. The sign disappeared.

The crowds continued to flock to the zoo to see its former star attraction. On Sunday, September 16, the number of visitors was estimated at a record forty thousand.

The Pygmy, dressed in his white suit and canvas shoes, now enjoyed the freedom of the park. In quieter moments he could be seen blowing on a harmonica and playing with a ball—often both at the same time. He wasn't hard to find, and the crowds followed him everywhere. Among them, unfortunately, were some of the city's roughnecks and good-for-nothings. They laughed at him. They howled. They jeered. Some would poke him in the ribs. Some would trip him just for fun.

It wasn't fun for Ota. He would run off. Sometimes the crowd would follow.

On one occasion, when a crowd was chasing him, he turned, set an arrow in his bow, and fired it at one of his pursuers. It hit a redheaded man in the face. Ota raced off to the monkey house.

The keepers, who had orders not to let Ota out of their sight, had their hands full.

Once a keeper asked Ota how he liked America.

"Me no like America," he replied. "Me like St. Louis."

As it turned out, the zoo's problems with Ota were just beginning. So too were Ota's with the zoo.

No one but Verner could speak Ota's language. The Pygmy's knowledge of English was limited—he understood only about a hundred words. Naturally the zoo's employees sometimes had a hard time getting through to him.

Ota, although often very agreeable, had a mind of his own. He had a clear idea of what he wanted, and what he would or would not do. His wishes and his keepers' often clashed.

One day, after Ota had been wandering about the grounds, the time came for him to return to his lodgings. With words and gestures the keepers told him to come with them. He shook his head vigorously.

The men reached out to seize him. Their large size and loud voices didn't cow the little man. He bared his teeth at them in a ferocious grimace. The sight of their sharp points made the keepers retreat in haste.

The zoo tried placing an African American in charge of Ota. He kept the Pygmy on the move much of the time, leading him into isolated wooded parts of the grounds. When Ota came back out, the new keeper ordered the crowds to stand back. A policeman was also detailed to protect him. That helped, but only part of the time.

Ota blows on an African horn that is bigger than he is.

Ota wouldn't mind if children or others teased him, provided the teasing was gentle. Tuesday, September 25, was unseasonably hot. Ota was laughing and fooling with some children. The keepers decided to add to the fun, and turned the hose on him.

Ota appeared to enjoy it. He started to take off his clothing. His dark wet skin glistened in the bright sun.

When he'd removed almost everything, the keepers decided he was going too far and told him to put his clothes back on.

Either Ota didn't like their tone or he didn't see anything wrong with removing his clothes. Angered, he ran off to the monkey house.

In a minute he was back. The big knife used to cut his food was gleaming in his hand. Weapon upraised, he ran at one of the keepers.

Maybe he meant only to give them a scare. But the keepers pounced on him and forced him to let go of the knife. Then they wrestled him back to the monkey house. Shoving him into a cage, they turned the key.

By now, nothing in the world would have pleased Hornaday so much as to turn the Pygmy over to the ministers. But the director couldn't. He'd promised Verner he would take care of Ota; without the explorer's consent he had to keep him.

At the end of the week after the first story appeared in the *Times*, Hornaday dashed off a letter to Verner:

> I regret to say that Ota Benga has become quite unmanageable. He has been so fully exploited in the newspapers, and is so much in the public eye, it is quite inadvisable for us to punish him. . . . The boy does quite as he pleases, and it is utterly impossible to control him. Whenever the keepers go after him in his wanderings, and attempt to bring him back to the Monkey House, he threatens to bite them. . . . I see no way out of the dilemma but for him to be taken away.
>
> It is my suggestion that he be turned over to Dr. Gordon and placed in the Colored Orphan Asylum. They have been insistent that they are the proper ones to take charge of him.

Hornaday kept writing his complaints to Verner almost every day. Sometimes they exchanged telegrams. From the explorer came a surprising piece of advice: If the Pygmy "should become too nervous, a dose of some sedative might do good, as I frequently found in the ecstatic frenzies which sometimes occur among the natives in Africa, though I never had to use any for him."

A sedative? If Hornaday were to try that and the ministers ever found out about it. . . . He decided not to.

Perhaps, thought Verner, he could calm Ota by writing messages to him in Tshiluba. Ota couldn't read—but he asked the director to read them out loud to his protégé. In one message he told Ota that there was a school in Asheville, North Carolina, that he would like. Would Ota be willing to make the trip? Verner said he would go there to meet him and get him enrolled.

Ota must have listened in wonder, trying to puzzle out the message as Hornaday read it to him. Maybe he grasped the meaning, and maybe he agreed to go. But how could Hornaday have understood the little man's reply in Tshiluba? And even if he had, how could he have gotten Ota to Asheville without someone to take him—someone who spoke his language?

Only Verner could help. Hornaday wired him urgently: "Boy has become unmanageable; also dangerous. Impossible to send him to you. Please come for him at once."

He couldn't at the moment, the explorer wired back. A tremendous storm had hit the region where he lived. His home was on a mountain, and the storm had washed out the roads.

Hornaday continued to tell him his problems with Ota. Every day brought a new one. The Pygmy had gone to the soda stand near the bird house and asked for some soda. The attendant wouldn't give him any. Ota, in a tremendous rage, started to peel off his clothing. An attendant rushed up and grabbed him to stop him from removing the rest of his garments.

"This led to a great fracas," wrote the director. "He fought like a tiger, and it took three men to get him back to the Monkey House. He has struck a number of visitors, and has 'raised Cain' generally."

In the last week of September Ota suddenly saw a worried, friendly face smiling at him. It was Fwela. The explorer had finally managed to come down from his mountain and return to New York.

Happy and excited, Ota poured out his heart. His troubles, Fwela told him, would soon be at an end; Dr. Gordon, a good black chief, had offered to take him into a home for young black people. If Ota agreed.

Ota agreed. He had some good friends among the keepers, and he quickly said good-bye to them. He gave them his arrows as keepsakes. To the chief keeper, his special friend, he gave the bow.

September 27. Brooklyn, the orphanage.

Dr. Gordon, his teachers, and the rest of his staff greeted their little brother warmly. Verner made a speech to Ota in Tshiluba, with appropriate gestures. This, he said, was the only place in the white man's country where Ota would be welcome for his own sake.

Ota's face lit up. He appeared deeply moved, and he delivered a speech in reply. The reception committee waited eagerly for the translation.

Ota, Verner said, had asked him to tell them "how happy he was to be with black people." He was also happy, Verner said, to be "free from the witchcraft of the white man."

For the orphanage Ota was very special, and Dr. Gordon had very special plans for him.

"We are going to treat him as a visitor," he told the press a day or two later. "We have given him a room to himself, where he can smoke if he chooses. We haven't placed him with the children in the dormitories, and he eats with the cooks in the kitchen." He had already made friends with them.

The orphanage had quickly begun the task of "civilizing" Ota.

With a pencil in his right hand and Dr. Gordon guiding it, he was shown how to write his name. "Ota Benga," the superintendent said, pointing to the words they had scrawled on the sheet.

"Ota Benga," repeated Ota.

Gordon made a suggestion. Ota seemed to understand. His mouth twisting with his concentration, he tried to copy the writing.

"That is a beginning," said Superintendent Gordon.

When the *Times* reporter called and asked Ota how he was getting on, he shook the newsman's hand and uttered a brisk "How de do!" In his pidgin English he gave the newsman to understand he liked his new home a lot better than the zoo.

The newsman packed his pipe with tobacco, lit it, and puffed away. Smiling, Ota drew out his own pipe and held it out.

"Baccy?" he said.

Who could have refused him?

Ota drew a shiny watch out of a pocket. It was a gift, and a very inexpensive one at that, but he displayed it with great pride. Next day, he said, he was to be given a new suit. It was obvious he was picking up the language of the *muzungu* fast.

The Hippodrome was one of New York City's popular showplaces, and the management invited Ota for a visit. (The publicity wouldn't hurt!) An automobile was sent to pick up him and Gordon. In the lobby, a baby elephant was distributing programs. Ota shrieked with delight.

Ota and the superintendent were escorted to a conspicuous box, so the Pygmy could be seen as well as see. He "gazed with awe and wonder" at a circus performance, reported the *Tribune*, and "kept grunting and muttering throughout." Afterward he was taken on a tour of the animal cages, where he watched trained bears perform.

False, exaggerated stories about Ota and Verner were turning up in the newspapers. Verner, in a letter to the *Tribune*, asked the public not to believe them. "We were simply two friends, traveling together," he said, "until New York's scientists and preachers began wrangling over him." He hoped Ota would rejoin him and return to the Congo.

"I saved him from the pot and he saved me from the poisoned darts, and we have been good friends for a long time. I beg New York not to spoil him."

It wouldn't for very long.

Every morning at nine, Ota was in his seat in the classroom with the other orphans. Pygmy though he was, he towered over most.

When the children wanted to leave the room, they had to raise their hands and ask permission. When Ota felt he'd been sitting long enough, he would simply get up and leave. Sometimes he would seek out one of the janitors and help him in his work. Or he might go outside to the high wooden fence and peep through the wide cracks. Sometimes he would make faces at the passersby.

Sunday meant Sunday school and, like the other orphans, Ota was obliged to attend. The Bible stories baffled him. He could understand them no better than the orphans would have understood tales of African myth and magic related in Tshiluba.

The hymns the orphans sang held just as little meaning for Ota. But Pygmies love to sing, and he joined in heartily, chanting at the top of his voice songs he used to sing in the Congo. Superintendent Gordon looked on, frowning.

To fit in with his black brothers, Ota was going as far as his freeborn African spirit would allow him. But that wasn't far enough to suit his teachers. He wasn't a child, like the rest of the orphans. He was a man of twenty-three, a hunter and a warrior. He had been twice married and twice widowed; he had been a father, and lost two children in a murderous attack. The son of a thousand generations of Pygmies, he had been reared in the rain forest, in an ancient, hard, utterly different way of life. His teachers, kindly, well-meaning, and deeply religious, had only the dimmest inkling of who and what he was.

The Pygmy in the Cage

If Ota had been an alien from another galaxy the Howard Colored Orphan Asylum might have had just as much—or just as little—success in turning him into the proper little black gentleman it wanted him to be.

The orphanage was discovering it had bitten off a good deal more than it could chew. Superintendent Gordon soon noticed Ota was making eyes at the older girls. His broken English became very fluent as he talked to them. And the girls were all smiles and giggles with this handsome, romantic stranger from the land of their forefathers, particularly an attractive girl who bore the colorful name of Creola.

Ota, although short of stature, Gordon realized, was a fully mature male. His moral code was definitely not acceptable to Baptists. Something would have to be done about the little pagan.

Far out on Long Island, the orphanage had another home, where older boys could take part in active sports and get work experience on nearby farms. Gordon decided this was the place for Ota, and he was promptly settled there.

Ota's friendly smile and manner won him a job with a farmer, who provided him with room and board and paid him for his work. He also became a star of the orphanage baseball diamond, keeping the boys in stitches with his high-spirited antics as he pranced his way from base to base.

And what was Ota's friend Fwela doing meanwhile?

In 1907 Verner was getting ready to return to Africa on a well-paid mission for the American Congo Company. He hadn't forgotten his little sidekick and his promise to take him back to Africa. But when he got in touch with Ota, the Pygmy said he wanted to stay in America for the present.

In 1909 Verner changed careers again. This time he took a post as a medical officer in Panama. A canal was being built there, and thousands of men in the construction crews had fallen victim to the dread disease malaria. Verner, who had suffered through many malaria attacks, was well qualified to help take care of them.

It was in Panama that a letter from Superintendent Gordon caught up with him.

Ota wasn't benefiting from the education the orphanage had been trying to give him, Gordon complained. Too independent. Too willful. A bad influence on the older boys.

For a while Gordon had sent him to a black Baptist seminary in Lynchburg, Virginia, where he'd had a great time and even been baptized. When he returned to the orphanage he was sporting, of all things, a Virginia drawl. But becoming a Christian hadn't improved his behavior. He was still a bad influence on the older boys—and Gordon wanted Verner to know the orphanage and Ota would have to part company.

Gordon's next letter announced that Ota had come to him and said he wanted to leave the orphanage. The seminary in Lynchburg would be a better place for him, he said; more people his own age there, and they liked him. Besides, he couldn't stand the bitterly cold New York winters. Dr. Hayes, the seminary head, had said he would be glad to enroll Ota as a student.

And so, on a teeth-chattering day in January 1910, Gordon put Ota on a train headed south and they said good-bye forever.

Life at the seminary was more to Ota's liking. He went on with his elementary education, but he wasn't held to any schedule. He did odd jobs for the school. He worked for local residents, who provided him with bed and board. For a time he worked in a tobacco factory.

The dense woodland around Lynchburg called to him. In it deer, rabbits, and wild fowl abounded, and such strange creatures as raccoons and opossums. Fashioning a bow and arrows, he hunted or trapped them with his age-old skills and cunning. Venison and wild turkey were delicious roasted over an open fire; Pygmies are sharers, and the friendly little man invited his new acquaintances to join in the feast.

Ota's African ways made a deep impression on his neighbors. Especially the young ones. He was fond of children—he had never gotten over the loss of his own—and a band of little black boys took to following him into the woods. He taught them his hunting secrets, how he trapped and fished, how he built a hut, and other woodland skills. He showed them African dances, and soon they were dancing with him.

"Ota Benga"—that was too foreign a name for Lynchburg folk. They Americanized it; he became "Otto Bingo" to them. He was a frequent guest at the home of at least two prominent members of the African American community, Dr. Hayes and a poet, Anne Spencer. If he was hungry or he needed a place to sleep, he could always count on them.

Although the little man made friends, he never could feel completely at home in Lynchburg. No doubt he liked it more there than at the orphanage, the zoo, the museum, or even St. Louis. But he was too different—an outsider, a man between two worlds.

For one thing, Lynchburg was the South. Every day he could see that African Americans were second-class citizens. They had to use separate drinking fountains, rest rooms, and eating places, and ride in the back of the bus. The moment they forgot who they were—or only seemed to forget—they could be beaten or tortured, or, sometimes, lynched.

Ota's thoughts turned back more and more to his home in the rain forest—to the excitement of the elephant hunts, the camaraderie of his kinsmen, to the precious family he had lost. By training and habit he was a nomad and a wanderer, unused to a permanent dwelling— always ready to move on, to follow the game as it went off in search of food. He had come to America with Fwela to learn the ways of the *muzungu*, not to become one of them.

Now he had learned as much as he could, or wanted to. He was an alien in an alien land. America had become a cage to him, and he longed to be free once more.

Early in 1916 people began to notice Ota was no longer the playful, happy-go-lucky fellow he used to be. He had lost his zest for hunting and fishing, for going out with his little band of young followers.

He wanted to go home.

But how could he? A steamship ticket would cost what amounted to a small fortune for him and, besides, Pygmies are spenders, not savers. His old friend Fwela had promised to take him back to the Congo, but where was Fwela? He had no idea.

Even if he could have found Verner or saved the money for the voyage, it had become impossible to travel to Africa. World War I was in its third year; German submarines prowled the sea lanes like hungry sharks, ready to pounce on any Allied vessel that passed. The Congo itself was aflame with war.

In March Ota discovered a way out of his cage.

A woman Ota worked for owned a gun, and he knew where she kept it. One day, when no one was about, he removed it from its hiding place and checked to make sure it was loaded. Taking it to the cowshed, he buried it under the hay.

After a while he was ready. Returning to the shed, he went inside and shut the door. He dug out the pistol. He placed the cold muzzle against his breast, over his pounding heart.

The roar of the gunshot shattered the stillness of the peaceful country day.

Ota was buried in a cemetery reserved for black people. If his grave was marked, no one knows where it is today. He was thirty-two years old. For a Pygmy it wasn't such an early death. In the rain forest few ever reached the age of forty.

Before long, Verner, still fighting malaria in Panama, heard about the suicide in Lynchburg.

"The news of Ota Benga's sad death inexpressibly shocked and grieved me," he wrote. "I never did thoroughly understand his mental attitude, but he was one of the most determined little fellows that ever breathed. . . . To me he was very human, a brave, shrewd, even smart little man, who preferred to match himself against civilization than to be a slave to the Baschilele. All honor to him for that, even though he died in the attempt!

". . . He left Africa because he would not be a slave, and he preferred to die in America rather than endure a confinement against which his spirit rebelled. The chains of civilization still were chains to him."

The Wild Boy

Winters can be biting cold in the south of France. There, on the morning of January 8, 1800, near the village of Saint-Sernin, in the department of Aveyron, a man named Vidal observed a strange figure prowling around his house. When he drew closer he saw it was only a boy.

But what a boy!

Except for the tatters of a shirt, he was completely naked. His body, thin as a rail and blue with the cold, was marked with many scratches, scars, and bruises. His black hair was long and matted. His movements, swift and furtive, were less those of a human being than of a wild beast.

From minute to minute the boy raised his head and looked about suspiciously, sniffing the air like a wild animal. Then, doubtless drawn by the smell of food from the kitchen, he hurried inside.

If he scented the man at all, he was too tired to run, or else the man was too swift for him. The door was slammed shut, and the boy was a prisoner.

Word about the capture of the boy-beast spread rapidly. Such a happening, in the heart of the long cold winter, caused considerable excitement, and people came from near and far to get a look at the captive.

The Wild Boy

The news soon reached the ears of the district commissioner, Constans-Saint-Estève. He hastened to Vidal's house.

When Constans entered, the boy was seated by a blazing fire. The room was full of visitors chattering around him. He kept glancing about, seeming very ill at ease.

Constans spoke to him. The boy made no reply.

The commissioner addressed question after question to him. The child didn't seem to hear.

Constans tried shouting. But that made no difference—the boy gave no sign he had heard.

He must be deaf, thought Constans.

As district commissioner, Constans was responsible for the wild child; he would have to bring him to his own house and notify the authorities. But when he tried to take the boy's hand in a kindly manner, the child pulled away.

How could he gain the confidence of this wild creature?

Putting a warm, friendly smile on his face, he started to caress the boy gently. He hugged him. The boy became less fearful. Finally he permitted himself to be led away.

The child looked half-starved. But what kind of food would a wild boy eat? Constans told a servant to fill a big platter with samples of all the foods in the house: meat both cooked and raw, wheat bread and rye bread, pears, apples, nuts, chestnuts, acorns, and other things, including potatoes.

As soon as the platter was placed before him, the boy reached for the potatoes. A fire was burning on the hearth, and he tossed them into it. While they sizzled, he examined the other objects on the tray. One by one he lifted them to his nose, sniffed, and put them back.

Turning to the fire, he thrust his bare right hand in, lifted out a potato, and stuffed it into his mouth.

"Wait till they cool off!" cried Constans.

But the young savage didn't hear or didn't understand. He kept gobbling down the hot potatoes hungrily, uttering sharp little cries as they burned his fingers.

He soon became thirsty. There was a pitcher of water on a table. Taking Constans's hand, he led him to it and tapped the pitcher. Wine will do this half-frozen creature more good, thought Constans, and he told a servant to bring some. But the boy would not touch it. When he was finally given water he gulped it down gratefully.

No sooner had the unusual visitor's thirst been satisfied than he jumped to his feet and shot out the door like a bullet.

Constans was right behind him. He shouted to the boy to stop, but he continued to flee. The boy was swift but Constans had longer legs and overtook him. The savage did not resist, and he was led back.

It didn't take long to discover the wild child wasn't housebroken. He relieved himself anywhere and everywhere, as soon as he felt the urge. "From his earliest childhood," Constans concluded, "this boy has lived in the woods."

The following day Constans had the boy taken by gendarmes to Saint-Affrique, to the orphanage there. Along with the child the commissioner sent a letter saying he appeared to be deaf and dumb, and he behaved like a wild animal.

Keep a close watch on him, he advised; otherwise he will surely run away.

For a month the savage was kept at the orphanage, while the government considered what was to be done with him. From the start, he gave his keepers trouble.

Any other child would have been happy to have a bed of his own. Not the wild boy of Aveyron. At first it was quite impossible to get him to sleep in one; finally, however, he got used to it. When his keepers put clothes on him he tore them off. After a while they hit on a solution: they clothed him in a gray garment, much like a dress, and fastened a belt around the middle that he couldn't remove. But there was no way they could get him to wear shoes and stockings.

The wild boy absolutely refused to eat the meals served to the other orphans. When some white bread was forced on him he spat it out. The only things he would accept were potatoes, acorns, and nuts. He peeled the potatoes and, it was reported, "ate them like a monkey."

The savage's eyes, black and very lively, seemed always to be darting about, searching for some way of escape. When he was allowed out into the field next to the orphanage for an airing, he immediately trotted off at top speed. His keepers, forewarned, chased after him and brought him back.

By now, news of the capture of the wild boy had traveled all across France and even beyond its borders. People's curiosity about him was intense.

One person who took a great interest in the boy was a highly respected naturalist by the name of Bonnaterre, head of a school in Rodez. The savage was transferred to his care.

The child, Bonnaterre thought, must have been lost or wandered off from his home years earlier. He invited people who believed the boy might belong to them to come and inspect him. Few came, and no one could identify him. It began to appear that he had purposely been abandoned in the woods.

Bonnaterre has left us an interesting description of the wild child. "In outward appearance, this boy is no different than other boys. He is four feet one inch tall; he seems to be about twelve or thirteen years old. His skin is delicate, his face round, eyelashes long, nose long and slightly pointed, mouth of average size, chin round, features agreeable, and he has an engaging smile."

There were scars all over his body. These could have been caused by mistreatment before he was abandoned, Bonnaterre thought, or else by animal bites and injuries suffered during his years in the wild.

When the boy raised his head, Bonnaterre saw a scar about one and one-half inches long across his Adam's apple. The wound could have been made by a sharp knife. Had the person who abandoned him tried to cut his throat, then had second thoughts?

The only authentic portrait of the wild boy of Aveyron. Note the scar across his upper neck.

The child, Bonnaterre soon learned, had turned up a number of times before his capture. The first time was in 1797, far away, on the other side of the mountains. He had been sighted by peasants in the woods near the town of Lacaune, prowling for food. He didn't have a stitch of clothing on. Before they could seize him he vanished.

A year later he was captured not far from the same place, brought struggling into Lacaune, and exhibited in the town square. When the townspeople relaxed their guard he disappeared.

In 1799, in the same woods, three hunters had surprised him. They chased after him and he climbed up a tree, but they pulled him down. Brought to town, he was placed in the care of an elderly widow. He was dressed and given kind treatment, but he never stopped looking for a way to escape. Eight days later he found one.

From time to time people would report they had seen the wild boy foraging in their gardens, or he had even come into their kitchens in search of food. Out of pity, they did not interfere with him.

At Bonnaterre's school the boy behaved like a wild animal in a cage. Sometimes he paced about on all fours, or, when he was sitting, he rocked his body backward or forward or sideways. His mouth shut, he stared blankly before him, his face without expression. From time to time his arms and legs moved convulsively.

He was a feral child.

"Feral"? The word is related to "ferocious"; it means "wild." Applied to a child or a domestic animal, it describes a creature that has been abandoned or that has strayed into the wild, where it has acquired the habits of a wild animal. There are feral pigs, feral horses, feral camels, feral animals of every kind—and, much more rarely, feral children.

Stories of feral children are as old as the hills. The most remarkable tell of children who were cared for by wild animals.

The best known of these stories is the legend of Romulus and Remus. Twin brothers, they were abandoned as infants in their cradle in the wild. A she-wolf discovered them. Carrying them back to her den, she nursed them with her own cubs. Later a shepherd rescued them. The boys grew into mighty warriors—not too surprising, since they had been suckled on wolf's milk. Romulus founded the city of Rome and became its first king. The figure of the she-wolf suckling the two little waifs is Rome's symbol to this day.

In 1341, in Hesse, Germany, a boy was captured who, according to reports, was also suckled by a wolf. He ran about on all fours and, because he refused to eat human food, starved to death.

In 1657, in the woods of Lithuania, a boy was captured who

**Jo-Jo, "the Human Skye Terrier,"
supposedly was found roaming the
Siberian steppes as a child.**

reportedly was living with bears. About twelve years old, he had scars over his whole body and moved about like a bear. In time he was taught to walk, but he refused to wear clothing unless beaten. Brought to the king of Poland, he was christened Joseph. He was put to work in the kitchen, carrying wood and water, but he never gave up his wildness.

Similar reports have cropped up all over central and eastern Europe. But they are greatly outnumbered by the sensational accounts of children reared by wolves in India.

No account of feral children has captured people's imaginations like the story of the wolf-children of Midnapore. These were two girls. According to the Reverend J. A. L. Singh, they were found in the jungle living with wolves in an enormous white-ant mound in 1920, and brought by him to a school he ran for orphans.

The girls, one aged seven or eight, the other about one and a half, were named Kamala and Amala by Singh. They lapped liquids like dogs and ate without using their hands, lowering their faces to the dish containing their food. They ran about on all fours, at the start, and their favorite food was raw meat. During the night they would give forth strange cries, as if calling to the wolves outside the orphanage compound. Neither child was seen to laugh or cry.

Singh and his wife worked hard to turn the wild girls into normal children. After a year Amala, the younger child, died. When Kamala realized her little companion was gone, she wept for the first time. During the nine years she spent in the orphanage she learned about forty words. She died in 1929.*

Reports of other children reared by animals continue to turn up. In 1945 the capture of a boy living with ostriches was reported in Morocco. In 1971 a French writer published a book about his encounters with a gazelle-boy in the Spanish Sahara.**

Was the wild boy of Aveyron cared for by wild animals? Some people said so—but no evidence was ever produced to support such a claim. However, he did behave like some of these feral children.

At Bonnaterre's school, for most of the day and all of the night, the boy was supervised by Clair Saussol, the school's elderly gardener. Clair gave him his meals and slept in the same room, and a warm affection grew up between them, although it was more on the old man's side. The young savage was housebroken—trained, probably by Clair, to go out-of-doors to relieve himself. Toothpick-thin when he arrived, he put on weight and increased in height. The boy attempted to escape four or five times but was always recaptured.

Interest in the young savage continued to grow. His capture had been reported in many newspapers, of course, but that was only one reason why people were so curious about him.

The time was a very special one. It was the Age of Revolution. In

---

*Singh's account of the girls was widely accepted in the West when it was published in 1942. Although in later years serious doubt was cast upon the facts of their discovery, the rest of the story was not questioned.

**Two feral characters of fiction have fascinated readers for generations: Rudyard Kipling's Mowgli, reared by wolves (in The Jungle Books), and Edgar Rice Burroughs's Tarzan of the Apes.

A contemporary but entirely imaginary picture of the wild boy. Note his long nails.

America the colonies had smashed the chains that bound them to Great Britain and won their independence. In France the long-suffering masses had risen up and savagely cut off the heads of their oppressors. The slogan of the day was Liberty, Equality, Fraternity.

A new era had begun—the Era of the Common Man. With it came a new philosophy, a belief in the natural goodness of humankind. Human beings, people believed, were good by nature. It was society—the old society—that had made them bad.

The French were intensely curious about man in a state of nature, primitive man. They felt a deep admiration for the Indians of North America and other "uncivilized" people. They called them "noble savages," made heroes of them, and wanted to know all about them.

With the discovery of *le Sauvage de l'Aveyron*—as they called the wild boy—Frenchmen felt they had found a noble savage of their own, an unspoiled child of nature. If this modern Adam could only be taught to speak, they reasoned, he could teach them much about the life of their earliest ancestors. They would educate him, turn him into a civilized man—and, as they did so, they could learn how the human race had developed.

The Wild Boy

One of France's most respected men of science now asked to have the wild boy placed in his care. This was Abbé Sicard, director of the great Institute for Deaf-Mutes in Paris.

Until this time, children who were born deaf and unable to speak had been cruelly treated. They had been considered worthless and useless, and had led lives of misery and abuse. But lately French scientists had been developing sign language and other methods to teach these unfortunates to communicate, and had been turning them into happy, useful members of society. Sicard was one of the pioneers in developing these methods. Who could be as qualified as he to teach the wild boy?

Other important scientists also wanted to see and examine the child. Lucien Bonaparte too, brother of the great Napoleon and minister of the Interior, had become interested. He ordered the boy brought to Paris for study.

And so, after five months, Bonnaterre and old Clair set out by stagecoach for the capital with the savage in tow. Actually in tow. To make sure he wouldn't slip out of their hands on the long journey northward, the boy was kept on a leash fastened around his waist.

People expected the wild child would be amazed at the sights, the wonders of industry and civilization he would behold in the busy

Abbé Sicard, head of the Institute for Deaf-Mutes, with some of his pupils.

cities he would pass through. They could hardly have been more mistaken. Only one thing interested the wild boy: a knapsack the three brought with them. It contained the boy's favorite foods.

Director Sicard waited impatiently for the arrival of "the phenomenon," as the newspapers were calling the wild boy. Sicard took pride in the extraordinary methods he had developed for teaching deaf-mutes. What success would he have with this child of the wilderness?

It took eighteen days for the wild boy and his companions to reach Paris. He had fallen ill on the way, and when they led him into the institute he was completely exhausted. He lay down on the floor and in an instant was asleep. Taken to a room with a bed, he soon fell into a deep slumber, watched over by the faithful old gardener.

The long-awaited moment finally came; at last Sicard could try his skill with the wild boy. The director took a keen pleasure in working with his deaf-mutes. He always found them alert, eager to learn, well behaved, grateful for the slightest attention. But the strange creature that confronted him, he quickly discovered, was as different from them as night was from day.

He was completely mute, except for a continuous harsh, throaty sound that came from him. When they tested his hearing—they tried many different sounds, from gentle music to loud noises—he showed no sign that he heard any of them.

Objects were placed in front of him. His eyes, unsteady and expressionless, wandered aimlessly from one to the next. He could not tell the difference between a real object and the same object in a picture. No one could detect the slightest trace of understanding or intelligence in him.

Pinel, France's greatest expert on mental illness, examined the boy.

The Wild Boy

The child, he found, was "without memory, judgment, ability to imitate, and was so limited mentally, even in regard to his immediate needs, that he has never yet managed to open a door or climb upon a chair to get the food that had been lifted out of reach of his hand. . . . his entire life was an animal existence."

A wild animal might have paid as much attention as he does to me, thought Pinel—and its habits would not have been as filthy or disgusting. Only two things appeared to interest him—food and a chance to escape.

Pinel was a familiar figure at the Bicêtre, a well-known institution for the mentally ill. He had examined the severely mentally retarded there. Did he see any difference between them and the wild child? None at all.

What should they do with him?

They could send him to the Bicêtre. But no, Sicard and his associates decided, they had taken him into the institute and they should keep him there.

Except when curious visitors asked to see the wild boy, he was left entirely to himself. Hunger would drive him to the kitchen, but otherwise he passed the endless, empty hours squatting in a corner of the lovely garden or hiding in the dusty attic behind some trash. When his keepers came after him, he fought them savagely and bit them.

The other children, who filled the institution, quickly discovered he was no one they wanted to be friends with. To make matters worse, some began to mock or abuse him—the same treatment they themselves had received only too often before coming to the institute.

If the savage had any feelings at all—and who on earth does not have feelings?—he must have felt abandoned. He must have missed the kind attentions of Bonnaterre and Clair, the fatherly old gardener, who had said that if the institute did not want the boy he would take him.

But of what the savage actually felt we know nothing.

■ ■ ■

To look after the health of his deaf-mute pupils, Sicard had engaged the services of a young doctor. This man was irresistibly drawn to the wild boy.

Jean-Marc-Gaspard Itard was a former army surgeon. Although only twenty-five, he was already becoming known in medical circles. His skill as a physician had won him the respect and friendship of the institute's director. Gifted with intense curiosity, a brilliant mind, untiring energy, and deep sympathy for his patients, in time he would gain an international reputation, as well as a permanent place among France's great men of medicine.

Itard had been present when Pinel and his colleagues examined the wild boy. Unlike them, he had become convinced the boy was not an idiot. Instead, he saw in him a normal child who had been isolated in the wild at an early age, and who had been damaged because of that isolation. The early years are the most important in our development—and the wild boy, living alone, without the affection and guiding hands of a mother and father, without playmates, had failed to develop the way a normal child does. Couldn't something be done by a willing young doctor to help him make up for those lost years?

The boy, Itard was sure, used only a small part of his senses and his brain. With patience and scientific ingenuity, Itard believed he could invent techniques to teach him to make better use of his faculties—to think, to learn, to communicate—to become more truly human. As the child made progress, Itard hoped, he himself would learn a great deal about how our ideas, our feelings, our abilities develop.

To Sicard, Pinel, and their fellow scientists Itard explained his theories about the boy. He outlined a careful plan for changing the boy-beast into a decent, intelligent human being. The scientists were impressed, and the savage was placed in his charge.

First, said Itard to himself, I must find the right woman to take care of the boy—a motherly woman, one who will look after him and give him the affection he has been deprived of. He found that woman at the institute—Madame Guérin, a housekeeper there. She was to be not just a governess but a substitute mother, a job for which she appeared well qualified, being a mother herself and a good-hearted, intelligent person in the bargain.

The savage would need a name, and Itard soon provided him with

Dr. Itard, the man who changed Victor's life. He was a pioneer in the study of disorders of the ear.

one: Victor. Victor was given a room over the apartment where Madame and her husband lived at the institute, and he ate his meals with them. While Itard was busy with his other duties, Madame Guérin was to be completely responsible for the boy.

Before he could begin to instruct a wild creature like Victor, Itard knew he would have to make the boy understand that he and the Guérins were his friends. He told Madame Guérin to give the savage all the food he wanted, and to allow him to do nothing at all if he felt like doing nothing. Victor loved to go out running on the institute's grounds in the snow and the rain; he also wanted to lie down and go to sleep as soon as it got dark. That was against the rules of the institute—but, from now on, no one was to stop him.

Until this time the wild boy had been sullen and withdrawn; he hated the institute and everyone in it. Now, suddenly, things had changed for him and he appeared more at ease. He would never go near the other children—he loathed or feared them—but, in an otherwise cold, unfriendly world, he had found three people who were on his side.

After some weeks this easygoing life had to change, so serious teaching could begin. But by then Victor knew he was among friends.

Games may seem like nothing more than pastimes, but they help to develop a child's mind. Victor did not even know what a game was, but Itard soon managed to interest him in them. Here's one clever way he went about it.

There is an old game, sometimes called the shell game. Three walnut shells are used. A small object, such as a pea, is placed under one of them. Then the shells are switched rapidly around, again and again. Finally the player is told to guess under which one the pea will be found. If he guesses right he wins a prize.

Victor loved chestnuts, so Itard used them in a new version of the shell game. Walnut shells were too small to hide a chestnut; instead, Itard used three silver cups, with a chestnut in place of a pea, and the chestnut as the prize. His mouth watering, the boy soon became expert in picking the right cup.

Next, Itard made the game harder; he kept adding more cups. But no matter how many he set on the table or how many times he switched them, the boy found the chestnut almost every time. Was that an idiot's behavior?

Itard's efforts, although often successful, weren't always so. Toys stimulate the imagination. Normal children love to play with them. To Victor, however, they meant nothing. He absolutely refused to have anything to do with them.

It was the same with the game of ninepins. No matter how hard Itard tried, he couldn't get Victor interested. The boy simply hated it. He hated it so much, in fact, that, one cold night, he gathered up the pins and flung them into the fire. That wasn't progress—but it wasn't idiotic either.

Victor appeared to be completely insensitive to differences in temperature; hot and cold were the same to him. This was one thing the boy would have to be sensitized to.

Itard began by cutting down the amount of time Victor was allowed to spend out-of-doors. In addition, he had him sit in a hot bath every day for a few hours. The boy played with the water like a baby, laughing gleefully when it was poured over his head.

As Victor got used to the hot water, he came to dislike the cold. He learned, before long, to test the temperature of the water, and he refused to get into the bath if it wasn't hot enough.

One day Itard and the governess tried to make him climb into a bath that was lukewarm. Victor, after testing the water with his fingers, had a tantrum. Then, to make sure they understood why he was so dissatisfied, he seized Madame Guérin's hand and thrust it into the water. Was that the behavior of an idiot?

Up to now, we have seen, Victor had objected to wearing clothes. If he were ever to become civilized, he would have to get used to them. On Itard's order, the fire in Victor's room wasn't lit on cold mornings, but he wasn't forced to dress either; his clothes, however, were placed close to his bed. Without the fire, the instant he woke up and threw off his blanket he felt the sharp nip of the cold. Before long he was putting his clothes on without urging.

Victor was a bed wetter. Itard studied his sleeping and toilet habits; then he had him awakened in the middle of the night so he would relieve himself in time. After a while the boy realized it was better to get up by himself than to lie in a wet bed. From that point on, he got up every night to attend to his needs.

The boy was completely unaware that he had a body and that it was made up of separate parts. He didn't know, any more than an animal does, that he had four different limbs, a head, a chest, and other parts. He would have to be acquainted with them. But how?

Massage should help, thought Itard. He set a time for the boy to be massaged regularly. As the massages progressed, Victor became more conscious of the parts of his body and what he felt in each of them. He also came to take real pleasure in his massages, and to feel affection for those who massaged him.

A Leyden jar was an early kind of electric battery. It was little more than a glass bottle coated with tinfoil inside and out, with a metal bar inside and a knob on top. The doctor used a Leyden jar with an electric charge to make the boy more aware of sensations.

First he had Victor touch the knob. That gave him an unpleasant shock. What would he do if he were threatened with another?

Itard began by forcing the boy into a corner. Little by little he moved the jar closer to him. He reached for Victor's hand; in a moment he was going to place it on the knob.

Victor was trembling. Suddenly, before Itard knew what was happening, the boy had grabbed *his* hand and pushed it down on the knob. Itard pulled back his tingling hand in surprise. But he wasn't annoyed—he was immensely pleased.

What better proof could he have that Victor wasn't the idiot that Pinel and the others had taken him for?

One curious thing Itard had observed about Victor: he never sneezed. It was an age when many people took snuff, a powdered tobacco that they inhaled, producing an exhilarating sneeze. Itard pushed some snuff up the boy's nose. Nothing happened. He tried again and again and again. Gradually Victor's nose became more sensitive.

Finally, for the first time, the boy sneezed—and was so astonished and frightened that he ran over to his bed and, shaking all over, threw himself down upon it.

Itard wasn't convinced that Victor was a mute. But when he attempted to teach Victor to speak he came up against a stone wall.

The doctor tried to get the boy to say the word *eau* (French for "water"). Holding a glass of water in front of Victor, he pronounced the word and then kept repeating it; he also had Madame Guérin repeat it. This they continued for quite a while, until—as Itard wrote later— "the unfortunate creature, tormented on all sides, waved his arms about the glass almost convulsively, emitting a kind of hiss but not articulating any other sound. It would have been inhuman to insist further."

Another word Itard wanted to get him to say was *lait* (French for "milk"). After four days of constant effort he succeeded. Victor often uttered the word when he was drinking milk; sometimes he would awaken in the middle of the night and say it. But, to his teacher's bitter disappointment, Victor never learned to say it to ask for milk.

Of the few other words the boy learned to say, two he was very fond of were *O Dieu* ("Oh God"). This was a favorite expression of Madame Guérin's, and Victor used it only to express great happiness. His pronunciation was never very good.

Madame Guérin had a daughter about eleven or twelve years old. Her name was Julie, and she came to visit on Sundays. Victor became very fond of her, and he would often repeat *Ili Ili*, with a note of sweetness in his voice. Sometimes he uttered this sound in his sleep.

In the end, Itard wrote, "I resigned myself to the necessity of giving up any attempt to produce speech, and abandoned my pupil to an incurable dumbness." He observed, however, that Victor could get pretty much anything he wanted simply with gestures, so actually he could manage well enough without speech.

The boy, Itard found, wasn't completely deaf. He could hear some sounds—especially those that had special meaning for him, like the cracking of a nut. The word *non* ("no"), which Itard said when Victor made mistakes, he certainly seemed to understand. And when his name was called he seldom failed to turn his head or come running.

If Victor could not be taught to speak, perhaps he could be taught to read.

Itard worked with him month after month, giving him exercises to help him learn to recognize the letters of the alphabet. Victor could not hear them or say them, which made the task much harder. But Itard possessed patience and a rare understanding of his pupil, and here too he invented unusual devices to help him. He even had the letters made of metal, and after a while Victor could identify them by their feel.

Finally, words. These Itard printed on pieces of cardboard; Victor had to learn to identify each one with a picture of the object it represented. The boy often became terribly frustrated and, working himself into a fury, would hurl the pieces of cardboard to the floor. Then he would run to his bed to fling himself down upon it.

Itard couldn't let him get away with this. Pulling Victor from the bed, he made him gather the cards and put them back in their proper places. He gave the boy no rest until he had done everything to his teacher's satisfaction.

Itard was not a hard-hearted man; his firmness did not last long. The result was that Victor's angry outbursts not only kept recurring—they grew increasingly violent. In his rage, sometimes he would bite the bedsheets and blanket. Sometimes he would run to the fireplace, knock over the andirons, and scatter the burning embers. When his fury came to a climax, he would fall to the floor and lie there writhing and twisting in convulsions that looked dangerously like epilepsy.

When matters reached this terrible pitch, Itard had to throw in the towel. This seemed only to make the problem worse. Victor's fits became more frequent. The slightest opposition could send him into convulsions. The doctor was worried. Was he, in his efforts to civilize the wild boy, turning him into an epileptic?

Something drastic would have to be done before it was too late.

Once, Itard recalled, Madame Guérin had climbed with Victor to the platform of the Paris Observatory. It was extremely high up. From the stone wall, or parapet, that enclosed it, one had a breathtaking view of the city.

Curious to see what lay below, Victor walked toward the parapet. As he looked down, he began to tremble. His eyes glazed over and his jaw dropped.

Madame Guérin was watching Victor with concern. He lurched back to her and, taking her by the arm, pulled her to the door. Holding her close, the boy hurried her down the steps with him, shuddering all the way. When they reached the bottom he began to calm down. Victor was, in a word, an acrophobe: he had an abnormal fear of heights.

It was this fear that Itard decided he would use to shock the boy back to his senses.

Soon enough, during a lesson, Victor ran into a problem matching words on pieces of cardboard and swept them to the floor. The signs were clear: any minute he would fall into a fit.

Itard was ready. Rushing to the window, he threw it open violently. Victor's room was on the fifth floor. Directly below were some boulders. A fall from such a height could easily be fatal.

His face a mask of pretended fury, Itard grabbed the boy by the waist and carried him to the open window. Turning him upside down, he thrust him out the window.

Itard held the boy there for several seconds. Then he drew him back into the room and set him on his feet.

Victor's face was white as chalk. His forehead was beaded with drops of sweat. His lips quivered, his hands shook, and his eyes were brimming with tears.

Taking the boy by the arm, Itard led him to the cards scattered on the floor. He told him with gestures that he was to pick them up and put each back where it belonged. Slowly and haltingly Victor obeyed, misplacing some of them. At no point did he make any show of resistance. When he had finished, he stumbled over to his bed and threw himself down upon it. His body shook with sobs.

In all the months Itard had known him, it was the first time he had seen the boy weep.

Itard's shock treatment, harsh though it seems to us today, did the trick. Although Victor still became impatient with his studies, he never had one of his fits again. Instead, when he was tired or frustrated by some difficulty, he would fidget and fuss, whimper a bit, and finally dissolve in tears.

If the lessons were hard for the boy, they certainly weren't easy for his teacher. Seeing how unhappy Victor looked sometimes and how hard he cried, Itard wrote, he was often tempted to "give up my self-imposed task and regard as wasted the time that I had already given to it! How many times I regretted ever having known this child, and freely condemn the pointless, inhuman curiosity of the men who first tore him from his innocent and happy life!"

To the wild boy, Itard knew, food meant more than almost anything in life. Why not widen Victor's taste in food—and through that his interest in the world around him?

With Madame Guérin's help, Victor was gradually introduced to different kinds of food, and in time he learned to like them. But not all. The candies and other sweets that children love he turned away from in disgust. Dishes that were spiced or seasoned he refused to touch, even when he was very hungry.

Itard took Victor to dine with him in town. On these occasions he had the table spread with an array of the boy's favorite dishes, which by now were many. The sight of these feasts drove Victor wild with delight; the first time, he even tried to steal and take home a plateful of lentils.

These outings soon became a must for the boy. Itard announced them with preparations Victor would be sure to notice: he always entered the boy's room with his hat on and with Victor's shirt folded in his hand. Victor fell all over himself in his hurry to get dressed, and he followed Itard out with a look of the greatest satisfaction. He grew so accustomed to these excursions that when too long a time passed between them he became sad and restless.

Madame Guérin also took the boy out for walks in the parks and gardens nearby. Because of the outings and the thousand and one attentions she bestowed on him, it wasn't long before he had developed a strong affection for her. Often he seemed sorry when he had to leave her, and he looked very happy when he came back.

Victor's attachment to Itard wasn't always so obvious, since much of the time the doctor spent with him was taken up with lessons that were puzzling or troublesome to the boy. Still, Victor appeared fond of Itard too, especially in the free time they passed together. In the evening, for example, when Itard came to the apartment just after the boy had climbed into bed, he sat expectantly, waiting for the doctor to come over and give him a hug. Then he would seize Itard's arm and pull him down to sit on the bed. Next he'd take Itard's hand and place it on his eyes, his forehead, and the back of his head, holding it there for a very long time.

Sometimes, when the doctor entered, Victor would jump up with a happy laugh and rush over. He would caress Itard's knees, feeling them and rubbing them vigorously for a few minutes; sometimes he would kiss them again and again.

"People may say what they wish," Itard wrote, "but I confess I lent myself without ceremony to all this childish play."

As we have seen, if Victor wasn't able to speak, he certainly knew how to make clear what he wanted by his actions. When he was hungry he would spread out the tablecloth and hand Madame Guérin plates, his way of telling her he wanted her to go down to the kitchen and prepare his food. When he was dining out with the doctor and he was impatient for his meal to be served, he would turn to the waiter or hostess and make a sound. If no attention was paid to him, he laid his plate next to the platter with the food he wanted and devoured it with his eyes. If he continued to be ignored, he picked up a fork and struck it repeatedly against the edge of his plate. If even this failed, he would thrust a spoon—or sometimes his hand—into the platter and quickly scoop the food onto his plate.

When the time came for Victor's walk with his governess, he would place himself in front of the door of his room. If she wasn't ready, he gathered up all the things she would need for the excursion and laid them in front of her. If he was very eager to go, he would help her with her hat and coat. When they were ready, he never forgot to put in his pocket a wooden bowl in which he would be served with milk.

In spite of the best efforts of Madame Guérin and Itard to teach him good manners, Victor was never a model of politeness. This was especially noticeable when he got bored or impatient. Sometimes people drawn by curiosity called to see the famous wild boy. When they stayed too long for his liking, he quickly let them know it. He would pick up their canes, gloves, and hats, bring them to the visitors, and then gently push them toward the door, slamming it shut behind them.

Somehow Victor's home at the institute, with all its civilized comforts, never felt like home to him.

Monsieur and Madame Guérin treated him like their own son. Itard gave him instruction and affection that money could not buy. But sometimes these things hardly seemed to matter.

Half of the boy's short life had been spent in the wild freedom of the fields and forests. No matter how long he lived in the city, he always felt a deep love for the out-of-doors. The howling of a stormy wind would fill him with excitement. The sight of a field buried deep in snow, of a woodland full of tall whispering trees, of a lovely bright full moon would make his eyes dance.

To this child of the wind and the sun and the rain, being shut inside four walls was like being locked in a cage. From time to time, memories of his life in the wild and his passion for the liberty he had lost would surge up and overwhelm him.

With Victor, at least in the beginning, to think of doing a thing was to do it. When his longing for the wild grew too strong he would run away, as he did that time at Madame Récamier's.

In his efforts to turn the wild boy into a civilized being, Dr. Itard would take him to social gatherings. Some of the most important people in France—politicians, ambassadors, generals, authors—might be present. One of these gatherings was at the home of Madame Récamier, a social leader famous for her beauty and intelligence.

It might have been expected: Victor paid not the slightest attention to his lovely hostess and her notable guests. They, however, paid considerable attention to him. To the wild boy, the only thing that mattered was the food; after filling his stomach, he proceeded to stuff his pockets with the good things on the table.

After a time, the guests became so absorbed in their conversation they failed to notice the wild boy had disappeared.

Then a noise was heard from the garden. Looking about, Itard realized Victor was nowhere to be seen. He rushed outside.

In a few minutes he located the boy's slight figure: Victor had stripped off his clothing and was scooting across the grass toward some trees. Tearing his last garment in half—his shirt—he climbed up in a tree as fast as a squirrel and perched there.

"Victor! Victor!" Itard called.

Instantly the boy leaped to another tree, and he kept moving from one tree to the next. He only stopped when he came to the last one.

A gardener joined Itard in his efforts to lure the boy down. He held up a basket of peaches. Victor could not resist.

In none of his escapes did Victor get very far. Except for the last one . . .

The walks Victor enjoyed with his governess and the doctor only partly satisfied his longing to be out under the open sky. When, as sometimes happened, an expected outing had to be put off, his disappointment was extreme.

The Wild Boy

Madame Guérin suffered from rheumatism. Once, when the pain became too much for her, she was obliged to take to her bed. She was unable to leave it for two weeks. Victor missed his walks terribly, but he seemed to understand why they were denied him.

When Madame Guérin felt well enough to get up from her sickbed the boy went wild with happiness. A lovely day followed, and he saw she was getting ready to go out. He got his wooden bowl and waited impatiently for her.

The door closed behind Madame Guérin. She had left him behind. His disappointment was enormous, but somehow he managed to contain it.

Then at dinnertime, as usual, Madame Guérin sent Victor to the kitchen to get the dishes. Looking out the window into the courtyard below, he saw the gate was opening to admit a carriage. In just minutes he was down the stairs and outside in the street.

Before long the boy had left Paris far behind. Mile after mile he walked on, tireless, headed north, searching. At last he came to a wood outside the city of Senlis. He plunged into it.

The wild boy had returned to his lost Eden.

But the past was past, he would soon discover. He was no longer the savage who had foraged for roots and acorns in the woods of southern France. He had grown used to the easy life he lived in Paris, to the meals prepared by Madame Guérin, to the warm fireplace, to his cozy bed and blankets, to the kindly attentions of his guardians. He was only half-wild now—perhaps less.

Edible plants, Victor discovered, were not as easy to find as they had been—and, when he found them, they didn't taste nearly as good as they used to. Sleeping on a prickly bed of leaves and branches had become extremely uncomfortable.

He felt hunger for the first time since he had been captured.

Hunger. He had almost forgotten what it was. Now he knew it was a terrible thing.

In the end, hunger drove him out of the woods. In the fields nearby he searched for a house, a house where he might find something to eat, as he used to do.

A policeman's sharp eye spotted the skulking figure. France, in the years after the revolution, was full of vagabonds, and houses were often broken into. The boy's clothes were dirty and torn, and his movements were far from reassuring.

A heavy hand fell on Victor's shoulder. Bewildered and frightened, before he realized what was happening, he was being shoved into a small, cheerless cell by rough-handed strangers.

For two weeks the boy, under lock and key, paced back and forth, howling at his captors. He was unable to speak, or to understand when he was spoken to, or to eat what was given him; and the way he behaved was, to put it mildly, peculiar. The police made inquiries, and finally he was identified. Gendarmes brought him back to Paris.

Madame Guérin came to claim him. A crowd of the curious looked on as the two were reunited. When Victor recognized his governess his cheeks turned white; he swayed and crumpled to the floor.

His faint lasted only a few minutes. When he opened his eyes, her arms were around him and she was kissing and fondling him.

Shrill cries of joy burst from Victor's lips. A happy smile lit his thin, worn face; his hands clenched and unclenched convulsively. To the onlookers he looked not like a runaway being returned to his keeper, but an affectionate child overjoyed to find himself in his mother's arms again.

Victor was just as deeply moved when he saw Itard. This happened the following morning.

The boy was awake but still in bed when the doctor entered. He leaned forward, his arms outstretched longingly.

But Itard was no Madame Guérin. He cared for Victor—cared for him deeply—but he was his teacher, and the boy needed a lesson now. His features frozen in a dark, unforgiving frown, Itard stood glowering in front of his wayward pupil.

Victor's arms dropped. He moaned forlornly and tears spilled from his eyes.

Itard wasn't finished yet. Although he knew the boy wouldn't understand a word, he scolded him harshly for running away. He raged on and on, his voice rising to a pitch of pretended fury. His stern looks and his violent gestures made his meaning only too clear.

Victor buried himself beneath the blankets. He sobbed long and hard. At times Itard could hear him gasping for breath.

He has learned his lesson by now, said Itard to himself. Walking to the bed, he sat down next to his pupil. ("This was always the sign," he would write later, "that he was forgiven.")

Victor flung off the covers and held out his arms. Itard hugged him.

Monsieur Guérin fell ill, seriously ill. He needed more attention than his worried wife, with all her responsibilities, could give him; finally he had to be sent to be nursed away from home. With gestures Itard tried to explain his absence to the boy, but he did not understand.

One of the small chores Victor had been trained to do around the house was to set the table for dinner. Now, although Monsieur Guérin was no longer there, the boy set a place for him as usual.

Madame Guérin, looking pained, told Victor with gestures to remove the setting. The boy obeyed.

But the next day he set the place for the absent man again. Once more he was told to take the setting away. He did so. The same thing happened day after day.

Monsieur Guérin's condition continued to worsen. In the end he died.

On the day of his death, Victor, as usual, laid the setting for him. As soon as Madame Guérin saw what he had done, she broke out in loud sobs.

Victor could not help but realize he was the cause of her grief. But did he think that he had simply done something wrong—or did he understand the real reason why the poor woman had broken down? For Itard, who was always trying to understand the boy's actions, the question was unanswerable.

Whatever his reason, Victor, with a look of utter misery on his face, removed the things from the table one by one and took them back to the cupboard.

Never again did he set a place for Monsieur Guérin.

Victor showed signs of deep unhappiness at other times, too. Especially when his lessons were giving him trouble.

His brows knitted, his mouth working, the boy would wrestle with a new word. Often it proved to be too much for him. In his frustration, however, he never blamed Itard for his difficulty. The fault, he appeared to understand, lay with himself—with his inability to learn some things. At such times the tears would gush from his eyes and splash on the table before him. To Itard, here was proof again that the wild boy was becoming more like a normal one.

There were other proofs, more and more, as time went by. One showed up during a lesson, when Victor had been driven almost out of his mind by a problem. Suddenly, without the least hint from

Itard, the solution dawned on him. A look of tremendous satisfaction spread across his face and he exploded in a huge burst of laughter. Itard praised him. Victor let loose a loud whoop of joy.

Itard was especially pleased when the boy showed concern for others. Before, Victor's only care had been for himself and his comfort, but now he was beginning to do things to help people he liked—Madame Guérin and Itard in particular. Sometimes he would do them even before they thought to ask him to.

Among the chores assigned to Victor, he liked best those that called for muscular strength. One job he loved was sawing wood. As the saw cut deeper, he would push and pull it with redoubled energy. The moment the sawed piece split off and fell to the ground he would cry out with joy. Physical labor was a welcome change to a boy who had to spend so many hours in lessons indoors. But he was also aware he was doing something that would please the doctor and Madame Guérin—as well as help to cook his food and keep him warm on a winter's day.

Victor's voice was growing deeper. The beginnings of a beard showed on his face. He was becoming an adolescent.

An interest in girls should be stirring within him, thought Itard. How will the wild boy react to it?

Like other boys his age, Victor became restless. For no apparent reason he was noticeably cross or moody at times.

"He changes suddenly from sadness to anxiety, then from anxiety to fury," noted the doctor. "He begins to dislike the things he enjoyed the most. He sighs, he cries, he screams, he tears at his clothing. Sometimes he goes so far as to scratch his governess, or he bites her." His face flushed, his pulse racing, he got so worked up that he had a nosebleed; at times blood flowed from his ears.

Victor's nature, however, was basically a sweet one. He soon returned to his normal self, and he showed every sign he was sorry for what he had done; the arm or hand he had bitten he would quickly cover with kisses.

It was, in many ways, an adolescence unlike any other. That did not surprise the doctor. Victor had no contact with other boys his age. He doesn't even know the difference between a male and a female, thought Itard. Although he stood in the place of a father to the boy, he had never brought up the subject of sex with him.

He hadn't dared to. Victor, while becoming more and more like a normal boy, still had much of the savage in him. Without the restraints bred into normal teenagers, he might have committed, Itard wrote, "acts of unspeakable indecency"—and just as publicly as he did anything else.

Blind instinct now drove the boy to seek the company of women rather than men. At a gathering where some women were present, Victor went and sat down next to one of them. Gently he reached for her hand and took it in his. Then he moved his hand to her arm and caressed it. Then to her knee. She pretended not to notice. The boy's pent-up emotions, instead of being relieved, only grew stronger.

Victor didn't know what he was looking for, but he hadn't found it. His face twisting in a grimace of irritation, he pushed the woman away.

He got to his feet, looked around, and walked over to another woman. Sitting down beside her, he went through the same performance as before, with the same results.

One day Victor became bolder. After caressing another lady, he took her by the hands and gently drew her into an alcove. Smiling, he offered his cheek to her and waited.

She declined the invitation.

His face turned gloomy and troubled. He offered her his other cheek, but now he seemed less sure of himself. Again his invitation was ignored.

Slowly he began to circle about her, on his face a thoughtful, wondering expression. Nothing happened. He moved closer. Suddenly he flung his arms about her shoulders, pulled her to him, and held her by the neck. This show of passion, like his other advances, was ignored. Shaking his head in annoyance, he pushed her from him.

From time to time Victor was driven to try the same maneuvers again. After repeated disappointments he gave up. Occasionally, however, his sexual side would reassert itself. He became restless and difficult, sad, or furious.

Whenever the boy's emotions unsettled him, his schooling suffered. Itard did what he could to provide relief. He prescribed baths, a soothing diet, vigorous exercise. Sometimes he bled him.* But any relief these measures brought did not last long.

In 1806 Itard's efforts to train Victor came to an end. In the more than five years he had devoted to the job he had changed the boy-beast into a human boy—not a completely normal boy, but one who was vastly different from *le Sauvage de l'Aveyron.*

At the request of France's minister of the Interior, he wrote a report on his work, recounting the great progress Victor had made. The boy still had serious shortcomings, he pointed out, but for these, he insisted, only he himself was to blame. He recommended Victor to

---

*Bleeding, or bloodletting, as it was also known, was used for hundreds of years in the treatment of many disorders. Usually the blood was drawn from a vein in the arm. George Washington was bled three times in two days during his final illness.

the continued care of the government. Itard's work was highly praised, and the report was printed at government expense.

Madame Guérin was asked to continue as Victor's guardian, and she was put on an annual salary. In 1811 a house was provided close to the institute, where the two could live together by themselves.

Victor and his governess stayed on there, year after year, taking their walks, visiting their friends, enjoying a quiet, peaceful existence. Victor never did anything that brought him to the attention of the public again. Virey, a naturalist who had studied the wild boy when he first arrived in Paris, called to see how he was progressing. Victor, he found, was still "fearful, half-wild, and unable to learn to speak."

Madame Guérin, if asked, might have said something quite different. True, Victor did not have the gift of language. But she understood him very well, and he understood her. He was not fearful with her, nor did she think him half-wild. She gave him all the love and care she could have given a child of her own, and he gave her the affection and companionship of a devoted son as long as he lived.

Victor died in 1828. Little notice was taken of his passing. Itard died ten years later. A highly successful physician, in his will he left a substantial annual sum to the Institute for Deaf-Mutes. His scientific contributions were many. He laid the foundation for an important medical specialty, otology—the study of the ear. He wrote the first major treatise on diseases of the ear and their treatment. He invented techniques to help the almost-deaf to hear better and to do something they had never done before—to speak. The methods he created to teach Victor and others had a lasting effect on the teaching of both the young in general and the mentally handicapped in particular. They also influenced Dr. Maria Montessori, whose methods of teaching normal children are in use in schools that bear her name all over the Western world.

Selected Bibliography

Bergsma, Daniel, ed. *Conjoined Twins.* New York: The National Foundation—March of Dimes, 1966.

Bogdan, Robert. *Freak Show: Presenting Human Oddities for Amusement and Profit.* Chicago: University of Chicago Press, 1988.

Bradford, Phillips Verner, and Harvey Blume. *Ota Benga: The Pygmy in the Zoo.* New York: St. Martin's Press, 1992.

Drimmer, Frederick. *Body Snatchers, Stiffs and Other Ghoulish Delights.* New York: Citadel Press, 1992.

———*Born Different: Amazing Stories of Very Special People.* New York: Atheneum, 1988; Bantam Skylark, 1991.

———*Very Special People: The Struggles, Loves, and Triumphs of Human Oddities.* New York: Citadel Press, 1991.

Durant, John, and Alice Durant. *Pictorial History of the American Circus.* New York: A. S. Barnes, 1957.

Selected Bibliography

Itard, Jean-Marc-Gaspard. *The Wild Boy of Aveyron.* New York: Century Company, 1932.

Kroeber, Theodora. *Ishi in Two Worlds.* Berkeley: University of California Press, 1961.

Lee, Polly Jae. *Giant: The Pictorial History of the Human Colossus.* New York: A. S. Barnes, 1970.

Meyer, Kathleen Allen. *Ishi.* Minneapolis: Dillon Press, 1980.

Shattuck, Roger. *The Forbidden Experiment: The Story of the Wild Boy of Aveyron.* New York: Farrar Straus Giroux, 1980.

Thompson, C. J. S. *The Mystery and Lore of Monsters.* New Hyde Park, New York: University Books, 1968.

Truffaut, François, and Jean Gruault. *The Wild Child.* New York: Pocket Books, 1973.

Wallace, Irving. *The Fabulous Showman: The Life and Times of P. T. Barnum.* New York: Alfred A. Knopf, 1959.

Warkany, Josef. *Congenital Malformations.* Chicago: Year Book Medical Publishers, 1971.

Young, Mark, ed. *Guinness Book of World Records.* New York: Facts on File, 1994.

Index

Index

Kroeber, Alfred, 39, 41, 42, 43, 44–47, 48, 55–57, 59, 61, 63, 64, 65–66, 77

Lambert, Maurice, 100
Leyden jar, 160
Louisiana Purchase, 120
Lynchburg, Virginia, 140–141, 143

MacArthur, Dr. R. S., 115–116, 128
McClellan, Mayor George, 129, 130
Madison Square Garden, 15, 16, 18, 24
malaria, 118
Meyers, Meyer, 88, 90–97
Meyers, Zion, 4, 7
midgets, 11, 16, 17, 18, 19, 20, 21; see also Doll, Harry; dwarfs; Graf, Lia; and Mite, Major
Midnapore, wolf children of, 150–151
Millie-Christine, 107, 108
Mite, Major, x, 16, 18
monkey house, 109, 111–114, 115–117, 128, 131, 132, 134
Montessori, Dr. Maria, 176
Morgan, J. P., 18
Mount Lassen, 48, 54
Mowgli, 151
Museum of Anthropology, Phoebe Hearst (originally Lowie), 43, 44–45, 55–58, 59, 61; see also Ishi
muzungu ("white man"), 119

Native Americans, 39, 46, 48–49, 52–53, 54, 63, 74; see also Yahi and Yana
New York Journal, 131
New York Times, 114, 115, 130, 131, 137
New York Tribune, 137, 138
New York Zoological Society, 130
New York Zoological Park, 109, 131
"noble savages", 152

Oliver, William, 95–96
orangutan, see Dohong
Oroville, California, 35–40, 77

Ota Benga, 109–143
appearance, 110–112
character, 116–117, 124–125, 127, 138, 139–141
early life, 117–118, 119
knowledge of English, 132, 137
at the exposition, 120–123
at the museum, 125–128
nickname (Otto Bingo), 141
at the orphanage, 136–140
suicide, 142–143
in Virginia, 140–143
wife, 119, 124
at the zoo, 109–117, 128, 131–136
see also Pygmy and Verner, Samuel P.

Pecos Bill, 3
pigmy, see Pygmy
Pinel, 154–155, 156
pituitary gland, 9–10
Pope, Dr. Saxton, 64, 65, 66, 67, 70, 75, 76, 77
Pope, Saxton, Jr., 67, 69, 70, 71
Pygmy, 114, 116, 117–118, 119, 120, 121, 122, 123–124, 125, 138, 139, 141, 143; see also Ota Benga
pygopagus twins, 80

Récamier, Madame, 167–168
Revolution, Age of, 151–152
Ringling Brothers and Barnum & Bailey Circus, 11–25
Romulus and Remus, 149
Rothbaum, Meyer, see Meyers, Meyer

St. Louis Exposition, 119, 120, 122, 123, 132
saldu ("white man"), 45
scalping, 49
shell game, 158
Siamese twins, 78–108
and identical twins, 79, 82
marriages, 101, 102, 103–104